Henry St. Cunningham

Chronicles of Dustypore

A tale of modern Anglo-Indian society. Vol. 2

Henry St. Cunningham

Chronicles of Dustypore
A tale of modern Anglo-Indian society. Vol. 2

ISBN/EAN: 9783337345099

Printed in Europe, USA, Canada, Australia, Japan

Cover: Foto ©Andreas Hilbeck / pixelio.de

More available books at **www.hansebooks.com**

CHRONICLES *of* DUSTYPORE

A TALE OF
MODERN ANGLO-INDIAN SOCIETY

BY THE AUTHOR OF

'WHEAT AND TARES' 'LATE LAURELS'

ETC.

IN TWO VOLUMES
VOL. II.

LONDON
SMITH, ELDER, & CO., 15 WATERLOO PLACE
1875

CONTENTS

OF

THE SECOND VOLUME.

CHRONICLES OF DUSTYPORE.

CHAPTER XXI.

MAUD'S SECRET.

In the glance,
A moment's glance, of meeting eyes,
His heart stood still in sudden trance—
He trembled with a sweet surprise.
All in the waning light she stood,
The star of perfect womanhood.

That summer eve his heart was light,
With lighter step he trod the ground,
And life was fairer in his sight,
And music was in every sound.
He bless'd the world where there could be
So beautiful a thing as she.

THE western horizon was all ablaze, and the
sun's rays came slanting through the gloom
of the Rhododendron Forest, as Sutton and

his companion rode down the mountain-side toward the plains.

Did Felicia's wishes and hopes breathe a subtle influence around them, which drew their hearts together, and opened to each the destiny which awaited it ?   Did the sweet, serious look with which she bade Sutton farewell speak to his eye, for years accustomed to watch for her unspoken commands, of something in which he had failed to please her, to understand her desire, to do or to be exactly what she wanted ?   Was there some shade of reserve, constraint, dissatisfaction in Felicia's manner that aroused his attention, and led him to explore his companion with an anxious curiosity which usually he was far from feeling ?   Or was it something in Maud ; a causeless embarrassment, a scarcely concealed trepidation, a manner at once sad and excited ; the flush that, as Desvœux had told her in the morning, gave her cheek more than its accustomed beauty ; which, before they had been ten minutes on the road, had sent such a flush of intelligence through Sutton's being ; which came upon him like an inspiration, clear, cogent, indisputable, and only curious in not having been understood before ?

Be that as it may, Sutton suddenly found himself in an altogether different mood, and in altogether different company, to that which he had figured to himself for the first stage of his journey. Maud had suddenly become supremely interesting, and infinitely more beautiful than he had ever yet conceived her. She was no longer the mere excitable romantic child, whose nascent feelings and ideas might be watched with half-amused curiosity, but a being whose brightness, and innocence, were allied with the most exquisite pathos, and who was ready to cast at the first worthy shrine all the wealth of an impulsive, ardent, tender nature. As for Maud, she was too excited, too profoundly moved, too much the prey of feelings of which she knew neither the true measure nor the full force, to be able to analyse her thoughts, or to be completely mistress of herself.

Dissimulation was an art of which life had not as yet taught her the necessity, or experience familiarised the use. The unconscious hypocrisy with which some natures from the very outset, perhaps all natures later on in life, veil so much of themselves from the outer world, had never occurred to her as a possible or necessary means of self-protection in an existence which till now had been too simple, childish, and innocent to call for concealment. She fixed her clear, honest eyes on her interrogator, whoever he was, be the question what it might, and he knew that it was the truth, pure, simple, and complete, that she was telling. Each phase of feeling wrote itself on her expression almost before Maud herself had realised it, certainly long before she knew enough about it to attempt to conceal it from the world. The feeble attempts at deception which the accidents of life had from time to time forced upon her had proved such absolute failures as merely to warn her of the uselessness of everything of the kind, even if it had oc- curred to her to wish to deceive. Her cour- tesy was the courtesy of sincerity, and she had

none other to offer. Those whom she disliked, accordingly, pronounced her rude, and
it was fortunate that they were very few in
number. Her friends, on the contrary, and
their name was legion, read, and knew that
they read, to the very bottom of her heart.
For the first time in her life she was distinctly conscious of a secret which it would
be misery and humiliation to divulge, but for
the custody of which neither nature nor
art had supplied her with any effectual
means. Silence was the natural resource,
but silence is sometimes more eloquent than
speech. Whether she spoke, or whether she
held her peace, Maud felt a terrified conviction that she would betray herself, should
it occur to Sutton to pay the least attention
to her state of mind.

' There,' Sutton said, pointing to a range

in the faint horizon, 'there is the Black Mountain, and there lies the pass where we shall be marching in a day or two. It is such a grand, wild place! I have been along it so often, but have never had leisure to paint it. This time, however, I hope to get a sketch.'

'Tell me,' Maud said, 'the sort of expeditions these are, and what happens, and what kind of danger you are all in.'

'I will tell you,' said her companion. 'They are hot, troublesome, inglorious promenades, over country which lames a great many of our horses and harasses our men. We burn some miserable huts, destroy a few acres of mountain crops, and drive off such cattle as the people have not had time to drive away themselves, and, in fact, do all that soldiering admits of in the absence of that most important ingredient of a brilliant campaign, an enemy—*he*, unluckily, is invariably over the hills and far away some hours previous to our arrival.'

Maud felt this account to be on the whole reassuring. 'How soon,' she asked, 'will you come back again?'

'Before you have time to miss me,' said her companion. 'It is an affair literally of days. Besides, Elysium, you will find, is all the pleasanter for having its crowd of soldiers somewhat thinned.'

'It will not be the pleasanter to us,' said Maud, 'for your being gone.'

Her tones took Sutton greatly by surprise.

'You are having a happy time here, are you not?' he asked. 'It seems to me a pleasant sort of life.'

'Yes,' said Maud, emphatically; 'the

pleasantest, happiest I have ever known. All life has been bright to me ; but there are things in it that hurt one, for all that.'

' Yes,' said Sutton, with a kind enquiry in his tones, for he had never thought of Maud but as the pretty incarnation of enjoyment. ' Well, tell me the things which hurt you.'

' The things that have hurt me the most,' said Maud, with a sudden impulse of outspokenness, ' are partings. They grieve me, even though I know that they are no real cause for grief. I minded leaving school, and my dear mistress, more than I can tell, and yet I longed to go. I minded leaving my friends on board ship, and yet I had only known them a month. I minded leaving you at Dustypore when we came away, and now to-day I am sad because you are leaving us.'

'That makes me sad too,' said Sutton,
grieved, and yet not wholly grieved, at each
new phase of sentiment which the childish
frankness of his companion revealed to him ;
'but, you know, we soldiers are for ever on
the move, and nobody is surprised or sad
when we are ordered off. You love Felicia,
do you not ? '

'Yes,' said Maud, seriously ; 'I feel a sort
of worship for her. Who could be so sweet,
noble, and pure without being adored ? But
then she makes me melancholy too sometimes, because she is so melancholy herself ;
and, oh, how far above one ! Could one ever
hope to be half as good ? She fills me with
love, but love with a sort of despair about it.'

  Maud was highly wrought up, and feeling
strongly and painfully about everything that
formed her life. She was full of thoughts

that clamoured for expression; and Sutton, she knew not why, seemed the natural and proper recipient; it was so easy almost to confess to him, to trust him with thoughts, hopes, pangs, which instinct said the common eye must never see; to claim from him a sort of gentle, chivalrous protection which no one but he knew how to give.

'Felicia,' Sutton said, 'need fill no one with despair, rather with hopefulness and courage about life. I have known her since she was a child; we two, in fact, children of two sisters, whose marriages had bound them closer in affection to each other, lived for years more as brother and sister than anything else. I have watched her for years gathering strength, calmness, and nobility from going nobly and calmly through the troubles of the world. She seems to me, in the midst of all that is vulgar and bare in the world around her, like the Lady in 'Comus,' impervious to everything that could sully or degrade.   But here, alas! our plea- sant journey together ends.   I must travel on alone.'

A few hundred yards below stood Sutton's first relay of horses, and here they were to part.   A trooper was waiting to escort Maud on her homeward journey till she rejoined Felicia and the children.

'This,' Sutton said, 'has been a charming ride, though something of a sad one.   I shall like to remember it.   See, you shall give me that sweet rose you wear, and that shall be my badge in all tournaments to come.   In return I will give you something to keep for me.   This locket, you know, holds my mother's hair.   I never part with it; but I have often thought it a foolish risk to take it on such wild expeditions as this. This time you shall take care of it for me, if you will.'

Sutton gave her the locket with the grave, pathetic air which, to Maud's eye, threw a sort of romance over his least important actions. He took her hand and held it in his own, and it seemed as though some sacred pledge were at the moment, with no spoken words, given and received. .

Maud never afterwards forgot that little scene, the kind gentle eyes, the sorrowful furrowed brow, the tender solemn voice ; in front the wide mysterious plains, stretching far below, all the horizon still aglow with the expiring glory of the sunset ; behind her a cold blue darkening world, the gathering vapours, no longer irradiated, settling in solid masses on the solemn mountain-tops.

As she came to a bend in the path she turned to wish her companion a last farewell, for she knew that he was watching her departure. Then she rode homewards through the gloom, moved, agitated, frightened, yet on the whole happier—with a deeper kind of happiness than she had ever known before.

CHAPTER XXII.

LOVE IS BEGUN.

Love is begun—thus much is come to pass.
The rest is easy.

SUTTON rode onward in a condition of happy
bewilderment. He recalled the conversation, .
every word Maud had spoken—her look, her
tone—and as he did so the result of the
whole seemed to take a deeper hold upon his
mind. An afternoon's ride with a pretty girl,
what was there in it to a man like Sutton,
the experienced companion of so many who
had both the power and the will to charm ?
What was there in this child, to whom he
had shown the mere ordinary good-nature

due to her circumstances, that all of a
sudden, he hardly knew whether by her
doing or his own, he should find himself
completely fascinated? How was it, too, that
the first woman with whom he really felt in
love should be so different from the ideal
which all his life he had set before himself of
what was especially loveable? In his child-
hood he had loved Felicia with the spon-
taneous and unconcealed attachment of a near
relation. Then had followed years of school,
long expeditions abroad, a life which soon
became adventurous, grave cares, anxieties,
and interests, at a time when most lads are
still trifling over their lessons. Sutton had
had not only to push his own way in life, but
to keep guard over others less capable than
himself, of whom he found himself, while
still a boy, constituted the natural protector.

His mother, suddenly left a widow, looked to him unhesitatingly for counsel, protection, and—so Sutton's account-book would have testified—supplies, which he was ill able to contribute. Brothers had had to be set a-going, and kept a-going, in that troublesome and anxious process of making a livelihood in a world where no one is in the least want of one's services. Then Fortune and Valour had combined to push Sutton forward as a· soldier, and one or two adventures, brilliant because they were not disastrous, made him a reputation, which secured him constant employment. When, years later, he had met Felicia again, a newly-arrived bride, in the Sandy Tracts, though he felt towards her the same affection as ever, it had not occurred to him to envy the man who was now lawful possessor of that to which he might have seemed, had circumstances allowed, a natural pretender. He had remained the loyal friend of both. None the less was Felicia the typical conception in his mind of what a woman ought to be ; her grave, refined serenity ; her unstudied dignity of form and gesture ; her mirthfulness flashing all about a melancholy mood ; her sorrows so acutely felt, so bravely borne, so sedulously concealed ; the prompt excitability that made the world full of pleasures and interests to her, and her a moving influence in the world ; the tenderness of sympathy which, beginning in the little home centre, spread in increasing circles to all who came within her range of thought or action, and enthroned her mistress of a hundred hearts, made up the type which his imagination had adored. Now he was startled to find himself kneeling at quite another shrine, adoring quite another deity, and adoring it, as he was constrained to confess to himself, with a sudden, vehement devotion characteristic rather of boyish enthusiasm, than of the mature sobriety of middle age.

Anyhow, as Sutton rode into the yard of the little inn where dinner awaited him he wished, for the first time in his life, that the campaign was well over, and himself safe back again at the pacific pursuits on which duty was just now sternly calling him to turn his back.

Here he found the Agent and Desvœux, who had been busy all the afternoon with despatches, and were waiting now for the moonlight to allow them to get forward on their journey.

Desvœux, as was always the case in times

of difficulty, had risen to the occasion, and fully justified the confidence of those who placed a seeming fop in a responsible position. He had been working all day like a slave, and he was now dining like an Epicurean, and in higher spirits than Epicureans mostly are. The Agent, who kept him in thorough order, and got an inordinate amount of first-rate work out of him at times, rewarded him by a generous confidence, and a liberty of speech in private, which no other subordinate enjoyed. A jaded, weary official, with an uncomfortably lively scepticism as to the usefulness of himself and his system to the world, forced into all sorts of new and uncomfortable conditions, could not but be grateful to an assistant whose spirits, like Desvœux's, were always in inverse ratio to the darkness of surround-

ing things, whose cynicism was always amusing, and whose observations on the world
around and above him, if frequently somewhat impertinent, were never without good
sense and insight.

At present both Desvœux and his master
were abusing Blunt over an excellent bottle
of champagne. Sutton was soon installed
at the banquet, which presently began *da
capo* on his account.

'We shall have no moon till eleven,' said
the Agent; 'so Desvœux and I are amusing
ourselves by inveighing against poor Blunt
for the kettle of fish he has set a-boiling
down below; and which you and your
troopers, Sutton, must dispose of as best
you can. It is another instance of that bane
of the service—zeal. Talleyrand was quite
right to insist on no one having any of it.'

'Yes, sir,' said Desvœux; 'Enthusiasm, Experience, and Principle may be said to be the three rocks on which we get ship- wrecked—enthusiasm, because it gives us affairs like this of Blunt's; experience——'

'Experience and principle require no illustration,' said the Agent, filling up Sutton's glass and his own. 'I feel how disastrous they are in my own case. But, seriously, one of the difficulties in dealing with a matter is that you always have to rescue it from the clutches of some one who knows too much by half about it, and who takes a host of details for granted of which nobody but himself has the faintest glimmer of understanding. You are right, Desvœux, in naming experience as one of your banes; I qualify it by the addition of an epithet— inarticulate.'

'Oh !' cried Desvœux, gaily, 'one takes that for granted. If men possessed the art of making themselves understood, there would be no difficulty in governing at all.'

'Yes,' said the Agent; 'officials and their reports remind one of cuttle-fish, beings capable of extruding an inky fluid for the purpose of concealing their intentions. And now, Sutton, king of men, tell us how you mean to lead the bold Acheans to the fray.'

'As fast as I can march the bold Acheans up. In three days at the furthest I hope to be well into the enemy's country—the mule battery will, I expect, do wonders in bringing about a loyal state of mind. And I may rely on the mules and camels for my commissariat ?'

'You may rely,' said the Agent.' I sent word to Boldero yesterday.' And Sutton knew that on that score, at any rate, he might feel secure.

'Boldero,' cried Desvœux, 'has no doubt by this time impressed every donkey in the province, and has a cavalcade of camels awaiting us. The job will, it is to be hoped, have driven Miss Vernon out of his poor bleeding heart. Here is to her good health.'

'And here's to Mrs. Vereker's,' cried Sutton, who felt an urgent need of an immediate change in the conversation.

'Cruel, cruel Sutton,' cried Desvœux, 'to suggest the mournful thought. Let me see : it is half-past ten. I left at noon. I grieve to think that I have been forgotten an entire afternoon. Mrs. Vereker's recollections, I believe, never survive a repast. Luncheon, no doubt, swept me from her thoughts.'

'Desvœux,' said the Agent, 'you are a

very unfeeling young man. I believe I am rather in love with Mrs. Vereker myself.'

'Then, sir, I presume you will wish me to transfer my attentions elsewhere; but meanwhile let me dream of the paradise I have quitted—

> In the clear heaven of her delightful eye
> An angel guard of love and graces lie ;
> Around her knees domestic graces meet——

'So that,' interposed the Agent, 'as you look at her face, and not at her knees, you naturally see more of the loves and graces than of the domestic duty.'

'Indeed, sir,' cried Desvœux, 'she is all that a wife and mother should be.'

'Very well,' said the Agent ; 'then go and order the horses, and let us be off.'

CHAPTER XXIII.

A STRAY SHOT.

A barren strand,
A petty fortress, and a dubious hand.

THE expedition, though in no way dis-
tinguishable from twenty others, did not
prove such a mere promenade as Sutton had
anticipated. The whole country-side was
in a nasty, excitable mood. The news of
Blunt's injudicious proceedings had spread
far and wide, and the prospect of endangered
rights turned the wavering scale with wild
clans, whose loyalty at the best of times was
anything but proof against a seeming danger
or a fancied wrong.

Every landholder whose title Blunt had impugned proved a centre of disaffection; and even where there was no reason for hostility the example of unruliness was infectious. Many a stalwart hillsman, coerced for years into uncongenial tranquillity, felt the old pulses throb within him, and, his heart beating high at the prospect of a fight, unearthed some primitive weapon, sword or matchlock or lance, from its hiding-. place beneath the floor of his hut, mounted on a wiry pony, and made his way over the mountains to the scene of action. Several more outrages, of which the District officers knew the significance too well, had already been reported. Everything predicted a storm, and a pretty severe one.

Indian life is like a strange, dark sea, full of invisible currents, strange tides, unsuspected and unexplained influences. The waters, which look so smooth and lifeless, may be stealing silently along and hurrying the hapless vessel to its doom. Magnetic streams, inappreciable to the nicest scrutiny, pour this way or that, and disturb the most accurate calculations; storms gather and lower and burst when all looks most serene ; a little cloud rises in the quarter where danger is least expected, and. in a few minutes the ship is tossing, a crushed and staggering wreck, in the midst of a tornado.

Just before the great outbreak of 1857 the ruler of India had occasion to remark on the absolute tranquillity of the Empire, and on the peaceful prospects of a reign which stood, as the facts proved, on the very crisis of its fate, and whose annals were presently to be written in characters of blood.

Men who live in such a world as this become
sensitive to its symptoms, and adepts at
interpreting them. The magistrates knew
well enough—they could scarcely have said
why—that mischief was at work. Police
officers on remote stations wrote uneasily,
and hinted at the advisability of reinforce-
ments. Strange, weird beings, whose un-
kempt locks and half-crazy visages bespoke
for them the *prestige* of especial sanctity,,
thronged about the bazaars, the wells, the
spreading tree where travellers halted for
rest and talk. A famous Fakir went through
the District haranguing excited audiences on
the kindred duties of piety and rebellion
against an impious ruler. Then the first
drops of the storm began to fall. One
morning the collector of a neighbouring town
was sitting in his verandah; in front a pair of

saddled horses were being led up and down; by his side was a tea-table, with letters, business-papers, and the frugal repast which ushers in the Indian official's day. At his feet two little children sat at play. From inside a lady's voice cried that she would be ready for a start in two minutes. Presently an animated bundle of rags, hair, and dirt came grovelling up with a petition. The misery of the creature was its passport, and the sentry who stood by, at a signal from the officer, let it pass. Then came a whining, rambling, unintelligible story of grievance; and then, as the listener's eye for a moment wandered from the speaker, a sudden rush— the flash of a concealed dagger—a groan—a heavy fall, and the Englishman lay dead on the ground with a cruel Pathan knife-wound through his heart. The assassin stood fiercely at bay, exulting in his accomplished vow to slay a Feringhee, and trying his best to stab the sentry who approached him. They cut him down as he stood, and before noon that day rumour had whispered in a hundred villages that Allah's will had been done, and that the Jehad, or Sacred War, was forthwith to commence.

To strike quickly, effectually, and with an air of absolute confidence in the result, is, in such cases the safest policy. A symptom of hesitation, an hour's delay, would ensure disaster. The spark, which one moment might be stamped under foot, the next would be a consuming fire, forbidding all approach. Sutton's business was, he well understood, to teach these lawless spirits (which no conqueror has ever yet succeeded in taming) a stern lesson of obedience, and to teach it them quickly, sharply, and in the mode most likely to impress the popular imagination. If all went well the business would be over in a week, and the refractory clansmen our good friends and subjects till temper, forgetfulness, or an official blunder, produced another outburst. If things went ill—but this is a contingency upon which the administrators of British India cannot afford to calculate, and which Sutton's temperament and good fortune alike had long accustomed him to ignore.

When he rode into the camp he found everything in readiness, and everybody in the highest spirits. Boldero had impressed a fine array of camels and bullock-carts, and organised a commissariat train more than sufficient for the wants of the expedition. The mule battery had arrived in perfect order. The little knot of officers who were to join the expedition gave a hearty welcome to a leader whose very presence seemed to them the best guarantee of success. In a minute the news spread through the camp that the 'Colonel Sahib' had arrived, and the men whom he had led so often to victory glowed at the thought that the well-loved and well-trusted leader was once again in the midst of them, and that something . stirring was certainly at hand. The little force was to encamp that night at the bottom of the pass along which, for the next two days, their route would lie ; then they would come to a high level table-land, where the enemy was (so the scouts said) entrenched, and where the serious part of the business might be expected to begin.

Occasions such as these were the parts

of Sutton's life in which hitherto he had felt himself most at home, and which he had, in fact, enjoyed the most keenly. He had been very successful, and had, he knew, been not undeserving of success. This was the thing in life which he could do pre-eminently well, and the doing it gave him a thrill of pleasure, which lasted all through the duller parts of his existence. Yet now things seemed changed to him. He had looked forward to this expedition with enthusiasm ; it had taken in every way the shape which he wished ; and now, when the hour was come, it had brought no sense of pleasure with it. Sutton was startled at his own lack of zeal. The lads who were having their first apprenticeship in actual soldiering were, he felt, far more soldier-like about it than he was. He could not sleep that night, and strolled

about the camp amid all the old accustomed
sights and sounds ; the long array of human
sleeping forms, each one motionless and
corpse-like ; the lines of tethered horses ; the
sentinels pacing stolidly up and down, and
challenging the passer-by in the still, clear
air ; the bullocks encamped by their carts,
serenely chewing through the peaceful hours,
undisturbed by the thought of pokes and
shoves which awaited them on the morrow. •
It was all very familiar, and brought back
many a like occasion of former years ; and
yet there was, Sutton knew, a difference :
the world was no longer the same ; a new
current of thought and feeling had set in,
and disturbed all the old associations. His
afternoon ride had metamorphosed his entire
being. Maud's sweet impassioned air as she
had wished him farewell ; her serious, soft,

pathetic tone, her last look as she turned to
go, the sort of earnest rapture which her eyes
bespoke, the unspoken pledge which had
been exchanged between them ; these were
the matters which preoccupied his thoughts,
and left but scant room in them for the
business which he had in hand. He found
himself, accordingly, uninterested, unenthu-
siastic, and, for the first time in his life,
completely sceptical as to the usefulness of
his employment. Every man, philosophers
tell us, is seized at some period of his career
with a misgiving as to whether his life-task
is not a delusion. Is it worth the long, painful endeavour, the patient waiting, the reso-
lute hopefulness which a successful career
demands ? Life seems, as it did to the sailors
of Ulysses, a wearisome, endless affair :

> For ever climbing up the climbing wave.

Is it certain that the end for which we struggle so earnestly is good for ourselves or for anyone? Sutton had such a mood just now strong upon him. He had been all his life soldiering; a hundred time-honoured phrases had declared it the finest profession in the world; but what did it come to? To be chasing a set of lawless savages about a country scarcely less savage than themselves, and inflicting a chastise-ment which no one supposed would be more than temporarily effectual. To drill a set of freebooters into something sufficiently like discipline to render them effectual as an instrument of destruction; to march up a pass and stamp out the first germs of civilised life by burning a few wretched crops and crumbling hovels; to fire at an enemy always well out of reach, and then

march down again. What was there in all
this to deserve the thought, the devotion,
the sacrifice of life itself, which men so freely
gave in its pursuit ?   Had not life something
better worth living for than this ?   Were
not the civilians right who sneered at
soldiering as a meet occupation for brainless
heads and hands for which, if not kept thus
wholesomely employed, Satan was sure to
find some less desirable occupation ?   Thus
it came to pass that of all the men who
marched in the expedition its leader was
the one who was least in love with it.

Two days later Sutton had warmed into
his work, and was in better spirits.   The
march had been delightful.   The splendid
military road which coiled in and out among
the folds of the mountain robbed the journey
alike of anxiety and fatigue.   Nothing gives a

pleasanter sense of power and triumph over nature than these great engineering exploits. You canter along a splendid road with easy gradients, a scarcely perceptible ascent ; there is a precipice above, a precipice below, and no spot anywhere on which, till the hand of science came to make it, a human foot could rest. Every now and then a distant vista reminds you that you are climbing some of the wildest and steepest hill-sides, in the world. The mountaineers may well cower and fly before a foe who begins with so impressive an achievement, and who cuts his way, resistless as fate itself, across the rocky brow of barriers which it seems half-mad, half-impious to try to scale.

The expedition, Sutton found, was in every way complete, His own regiment was always ready to march at twenty minutes'

notice, and the General at Dustypore seemed
to have been equally well prepared.   The
air, despite the hot sun, was fresh and
exhilarating; the men in the very mood for
brilliant service.   Besides, a peasant who had
just been brought in from the District told
them that, ten miles across the plain which
now stretched away in gentle undulations
before them, the enemy was entrenched in
strength, and intended to show fight.   The
village had been fortified, the man said, with
a wall of earth and stones, and the fighters
would be found behind it.

'Then, gentlemen,' cried Sutton, who
was standing with a knot of officers at his
tent-door when the news arrived, 'I propose
that we attack them to-night.   If we let
them have a day to do it in, these scoundrels
will give us the slip.'

In half an hour the whole force was on the march. The day was delightfully fresh ; the mountain-mists gathered overhead, and formed a welcome shelter from the blazing sky. Sutton had his troopers on either flank ; then came the tiny battery, looking more like playthings than the grim realities the Armstrongs proved, in the midst of a long line of Native Infantry. The men marched with a will, and with the exciting conscious‑ness that in the afternoon there was to be a fight. At noon, when there was a halt to rest the force, the outline of the village-wall might be clearly seen, and those who had telescopes could make out an occasional figure creeping stealthily about. There was a little rising ground some half-mile from the village, and here Sutton determined to establish his battery. The tiny telescope-

like tubes soon did the work, and the main
gate of the village fell inwards with a crash,
the mud wall crumbled and fell wherever it
was touched, and a thick cloud of dust
showed where each ball had lodged.   In
ten minutes the village was in flames, and
Sutton's little army was advancing on it at
a run.   Presently they got within musket-
shot, and bullet after bullet came singing
through the air.   Sutton was riding, with a
trumpeter on the right, half-a-dozen yards in
advance of his men ; the ground, though
firm and safe, grew rougher as they neared
the village, and the troops' line was somewhat broken.   By this time they could make
out the mud-wall which had been thrown up
in front of the village and measure the paces
between it and them.   It was a mere nothing, but the men were going at it faster

than they should. Two horses were struck and fell heavily just as their riders were pulling them together for the jump. Half-a-dozen more refused—then came the usual scene of rearing, plunging, and dismounted men. There was an instant's check, but only an instant's, for Sutton and the trumpeter were over, and the first dozen men who followed them had knocked the wall level with the ground. Sutton had speedily dis-. posed of two of the hillsmen, who fired their pistols in his face and made at him with their swords ; and had galloped up to help the trumpeter, who was having a hard time of it with a Sowar, mounted on a nimble little horse, and evidently a competent and prac-tised swordsman. The man turned on his noble antagonist, and made a cut which left a deep dent on Sutton's sword-handle. The native had, however, met with more than his match. The others got over just in time to see Sutton cut him down, and his horse gallop wildly off with an empty saddle. The men gave a shout and galloped forward. Then some one from a neighbouring window took a lucky shot. Sutton was at the moment giving an order, and pointing with his sword in the direction indicated. His sword flew out of his hand, his arm fell powerless, and his horse, rearing up, fell back upon him. His native aide-de-camp dragged him out from under the horse, which was lying shot through the heart across him. Half-a-dozen men carried him to the rear. Ten minutes later, when the village had been cleared, and the troop returned from the pursuit, they found him lying in a crimson pool, insensible, with a broken arm and a bullet-wound in his side, the red stream from which the surgeon, kneeling beside him, was endeavouring in vain to staunch.

CHAPTER XXIV.

THE GULLY.

I know not if I know what true love is ;
But if I know, then if I love not him,
Methinks there is none other I can love.

PERHAPS the thing which more than any
other exasperated Fotheringham about this
unlucky frontier outbreak was the cool way
in which Blunt took it. He quite ignored
all responsibility in the matter. This was
more than Fotheringham could forgive.
When he had to come post-haste back to
Dustypore, with his tail, so to speak, between
his legs, leaving the country in a blaze behind
him, with an escort of cavalry to protect him

from the animosities which his proceedings
had provoked, the least that could be expected of him was to wear the penitent air
of a man who has had his own way and
come to grief. Blunt, however, was as un-
abashed and uncompromising as before, and
it had never, it was evident, crossed his mind
that he could be the person to blame. The
whole affair was gall and wormwood to
Fotheringham : it was improper, incongru-.
ous, and a shock to his perceptions of the
eternal fitness of things. It never ought to
have happened—never, so his fine instincts
told him, would have happened—but for this
rough, self-confident, inexperienced outsider.
It came too at the most horrid time of year,
just when almost everyone was at the hills,
and the few whose ill-luck compelled them
to remain in the plains were exhausted with

the summer, and in need of repose. The Misses Fotheringham and their mamma had been all the summer at Elysium, and poor Fotheringham had been meaning to join them for a few weeks' autumnal holiday, and this was now out of the question. This in itself was no small grievance. And then, on public grounds, Fotheringham felt the outbreak a sort of stain on himself and the institution which he cared most about. The Salt Board might be to others a mere ab-straction, but he had worked at it and in it till he had come to regard it with a sort of fondness. Now, Blunt's mismanagement exhibited the Board in a perfectly false light, as political incendiaries. The Rumble Chunder Grant was made to figure as a stone of stumbling and rock of political offence, instead of, as its advocates felt it to be, a sort of moral buffer on which any little unpleasantness which the wear and tear of government engendered, was allowed to vent itself in safety. Fotheringham had exactly foretold the result, and felt, it must be supposed, that kind of melancholy satisfaction which the most good-natured prophets of evil cannot but experience when their prophecies come true. He was too much of a gentleman to say to Blunt, ' There ! I told you so, in so many words ;' but this was what he *felt*, and this sort of inward triumph joined together with the other and graver aspects of the affair to make him treat Blunt in a manner, which, no doubt, the latter gentleman, pachydermatous as he was, found the reverse of soothing.

Cockshaw, too, in his idle way, was greatly put out, and not at all inclined to

make himself pleasant. He smoked more
cheroots than ever, was more impatient of
discussion, fidgeted worse when Fotheringham was settling down into nicely-rounded
periods, and getting real relief from doing so,
and altogether did not behave as Fotheringham felt that he ought at a trying time.

Of his two colleagues Cockshaw had
come to dislike Blunt by far the worst.
Fotheringham, he knew, was an ass; but
then he had known him as such ever since
they were at Haileybury together as lads,
and his being asinine seemed all right and
proper in the natural course of things. With
all his feebleness he had a sort of chivalry
about him, a pride in his order, an enthusiasm
about his work, a professional sympathy
with his colleagues, which bound him to his
brother-civilians. Blunt was a stranger to
all this, and was known to talk about the

Civil Service in a way that made Cockshaw
long to knock him down, and give him a
thrashing, as he would have done to a rude
schoolfellow years ago. An article appeared
in the 'Edinburgh Review' about the
Government of India, which Cockshaw felt
certain from its style was Blunt's, and which
spoke of the administrators of the country
with undisguised contempt. There was a
phrase about 'one dead level of mediocrity,'
which some angry Governor-General had
used, and which the article quoted with
an approval which Cockshaw could neither
forgive nor forget. The Rumble Chunder
Grant was quoted as a specimen of the
gigantic messes which ensue, when second
and third rate men have the management
of first-rate questions. The local Governments were described as costly bureaux,

with all the natural defects of a bureau and
some peculiar evils of their own to boot—
now meddlesome and fussy, now indolent and
obstructive, frequently unprincipled and in-
subordinate. The three separate War estab-
lishments were disposed of with a sneer as
the most expensive folly in existence. The
vile corruption which characterised the East
India Company in its earlier days, the
scandalous exhibitions of public and private
wickedness which fired the righteous wrath
of Burke, had, the writer admitted, been
rendered impossible by the increased com-
munication with home, and the generally
improved tone of English manners ; but
Indian Governments had long remained the
home of jobbery. The stringent remedy of
the Competitive System had been necessary
to deal with the accumulated dulness with

which years of licensed favouritism had crowded the ranks of the service. On the whole it was not true, or any thing like true, that India was well administered. The wonder, however, was, considering the class of men to whom the job had been entrusted, that it had ever got administered at all.

' D—— his impudence !' exclaimed Cockshaw, with all the fervour of an indignation which had been gaining strength through a dozen pages of unpalatable reading ; and the expression may be taken as representing in a concise formula the view which Cockshaw had come to take of his colleague's mental altitude, and of the respect or consideration to which he and his proposals were entitled.

The meetings of the Board grew very stern and stiff. Unluckily, too, at this very time the Board's Annual Report had to be written, and the conflicting views of the members as to the cause of the disaster could scarcely fail to be brought prominently forward. It was one of the occasions which Strutt had been accustomed to treat historically, and which called, he felt, for something grander than Whisp's business-like and unpretentious style. 'My good sir,' he would say, 'I have no time to read history : I am *making* it.' In the good old days, when Strutt had his own way, he would have knocked the affair off in half-a-dozen well-rounded, vague, magniloquent phrases ; have left the connection of the Board with the whole thing in obscurity ; have congratulated the Government on the excellent behaviour of the troops ; and paid Providence a handsome compliment on the fortunate turn which events had taken.

But now Strutt felt a painful misgiving
that this sort of thing would not do. When
he began the paragraph—' The sun of the
official year has set in blood,' he saw Blunt's
horrid cynical look, and knew that he would
never stand it. Any allusion to Providence—
and Strutt felt that one was quite essential
to anything like a proper peroration—Blunt
would, he was sure, ruthlessly draw his pen
through.   Nor was it only as to matters of
taste and style that Strutt felt embarrassed.
Fotheringham would, he was certain, depre-
cate any reference to a connection between
the outbreak and the Rumble Chunder
Grant. ' Policy,' he would say, in a mysterious way, ' calls for reticence. We may be
misconstrued, but we cannot afford to show
all the world our hand; we don't want the
hillmen to imagine that we admit them to

have a grievance.' Blunt, on the other hand, would be for having it all down in black and white—for describing the outbreak as the natural result of indistinctness, cowardice, and idleness. Altogether Strutt felt that his lines had been cast in rough places, and began to agree with Fotheringham that outsiders like Blunt were a mistake.

While things stood thus, one of those events occurred which form so constant a characteristic of Indian life, and add so formidable a contribution to the difficulties of government. How is it possible to have continuity of action, settled policy, completeness of design, when existence is so shifting that no man who begins a work is likely to see its close ? Promotion, or leave, or the chances of health keep the hierarchy of Indian officials for ever on the move. One

man goes home to Europe, and his departure involves the change of a dozen men,
each of whom is waiting anxiously for an
advance, and is entitled to step into his
fellow's shoes.   One of these vicissitudes
befell the Board, for poor Fotheringham fell
violently ill, and for some time seemed likely
to create a permanent vacancy.   A week's
fever left him a skeleton, but a live one, and
his only chance of re-established health was
immediate flight for home.   Accordingly, in
fewer hours than it takes an English lady
days to determine where she will spend her
summer holiday the Fotheringham establishment had moved off the scene.   The fine
barouche—the Australian carriage-horses—
the lovely Arabs on which the Misses Fotheringham took their morning exercise—the
pretty garden where their mamma received

society to tea and croquet—the dining-room where the Senior Member had regaled his friends—the library where he assailed his enemies—the piano at which the young ladies sang tremendous duets—the arm-chair in which Fotheringham had sate and thought, or seemed to think—all became matters of the past.   A neat paper, copied out by the elder Miss Fotheringham, and containing the scanty catalogue of an Indian official's worldly belongings, was circulated in the station, each item at so many rupees for those who liked to buy.   Before the week was over the house was stripped, the simple treasures were scattered to a dozen new possessors, and the Fotheringhams, as the Arab folds his tent and slides silently away, had departed.   The waters of official life rolled smoothly over them, and next day the

' Dustypore Gazette ' announced with laconic severity that Mr. Snaply had on such and such a morning taken over charge, as Member of the Revenue Board, from Mr. Fotheringham, during the absence of the latter on sick leave, or pending further orders.

Now, Snaply was known as the crossest man in the ' Service,' and it cheered poor Fotheringham, who was almost too ill and weak to care about anything, to know that his *locum tenens* would not allow Blunt to repose on a bed of roses if he could help it.

Felicia, meanwhile, had carried Maud off to the 'Gully,' a mountain retreat some twenty miles away, where purer air and a less constrained life were to be had than at Elysium. It was, in fact, nothing more than one of a cluster of log-huts, built years before, when a working party of soldiers had been cutting one of the grand military roads that traverse the mountains in these parts, and sold off-hand, when the work was done, for what they would fetch to the first comer. Felicia and her husband had been encamped in the neighbourhood, and had fallen in love with the wildness of the place, the exquisitely pure air, the huge towering pines, which gave the scene a character of its own, and, more-over, with the unfamiliar idea of owning a part of the Himalayas in freehold. For a few hundred rupees, accordingly, Vernon had become possessor of the huts and some adjoining acres, and since then Felicia's embellishing hand had worked wonders. Nature, as if in gratitude for unaccustomed devotion, lent herself in a lavish mood to beautify the little structure. A profuse

growth of creepers festooned the porch; a
delicious piece of turf, bright, smooth, and
soft, and broken only by one or two project-
ing crags, stretched down the mountain-side
in front; and inside the rough deodar paling
the beds were all ablaze with English flowers
that not even Felicia's tenderness could coax
into healthiness in the plain below. 'These
are my invalids,' Felicia said, to whom this
spot was always full of charm. 'I send
them up with the babies to breathe a little
wholesome air. Shut your eyes, Maud, and
smell this—cannot you fancy yourself in a
sweet English wood in June?' There were
other beauties, moreover, about the place
than those of an English summer. They
were hanging in a little picturesque nook of
safety, but all around them was sublime.
Storms gathered and crashed and spent their

fury as if this was their very home where
they could play at ease. An inky mass
came lowering over the heights above and
shed itself in one angry deluge on the
mountain-side, the thunder crashed in fierce
echoes from crag to crag, and all the heavens
blazed from end to end as the fearful fiery
zig-zags came darting out of the gloom; then
the tempest would pass away and nothing
be heard but the distant rumble and the
hundred muddy torrents roaring downwards.
The great folds of mist came swirling up
the precipice, wrapping everything for a few
moments in gloom; then they would pass on,
and presently again the sky be serene and
bright, and the reeking mountains sun
themselves gleefully in the brightness and
warmth that were everywhere present.

'It is beautiful,' Maud said, 'but too

grand to be quite pleasant ; it is rather awful. That black mountain opposite, with its army of skeleton deodars, makes me shudder.'

Across the gorge the forest had been burnt—the first rude attempt by the mountaineers at reclaiming the soil. For weeks together these blazing patches may be seen on the hillside, hidden in a cloud of smoke by day, and at night lighting up the landscape with a lurid, fitful glare. When, by a change in the wind or sudden downpour, the conflagration ceases, nothing remains but a gloomy array of charred stumps, with here and there some monstrous stem towering above, which the flames, though they were able to kill, have not succeeded in devouring. Then among the ruins of the forest comes the primitive cultivator, with his tiny plough and scrambling goat-like bullocks, and wrings a scanty crop of oats or potatoes from each ridge and cranny of the rocky steep ; and so the reign of agriculture has begun. The effect, however, from the picturesque point of view is weird and gloomy ; it was so, at any rate, in Maud's thoughts, for she ever after associated it with the first piece of really bad news that had ever come to her in the whole of her sunshiny existence. A note arrived one morning from Vernon at Dustypore, and Felicia read it out before she was well aware of its import. He was just starting, Vernon said, for the head-quarters of the expedition. 'There has been a fight, and the entrenched village has been carried by a *coup de main*, and——'

'And what ?' said Maud, who felt herself turning deadly cold, and her heart beating

so that she could scarcely speak. ' Go on,
Felicia, please.'

' " Sutton, I fear, has had a serious wound,
and a fall from his horse. I am going out
to look after him. More news to-morrow." '

Maud rose and fled, without a word, to
her bedroom, to deal with this agitating
piece of news as best she might. She did
not feel sure enough of her composure to
trust herself to the chances of a break-down .
even before Felicia. There was something
in herself, she knew, that she did not wish
even Felicia's eye to read. To Felicia her
husband's letter spoke only of the fortunes
of their common friend ; to Maud it was, as a
quick, agonising pang told her, an affair of
life or death. A serious wound—a fall from
horseback—terrible, vague words that might
mean anything—that might mean something

that would eclipse all Maud's existence in the gloom of a lifelong disaster. She had thought over their last ride together often; but she knew now, and now only, to the full what it had really been to her. She had recalled his last acts and words—they had been sweet and tender words, such as would keep their fragrance through a lifetime; but, supposing that they were to be really last words, the long farewell of a man who was going to his doom! Maud sat still, crushed and stunned at this first brush of misfortune's passing wing—a dark shadow, black and fateful as the storms which came raging up the valley, seemed to be gathering across her life. Life itself seemed to hang on a slender thread, the tidings which to-morrow's messenger should bring—perhaps even now life was over for her.

Felicia did not leave her long in solitude; she came in presently, with her kind, considerate air, knowing and feeling all, as Maud instinctively was aware, but speaking only just what should be spoken, and guarded by a delicate tact, rare attribute of ·only the most finely-moulded natures, from the possibility of a word too much.

'Courage,' she said; 'I know the meaning of George's letter too well to be frightened. . To-morrow, dear Maud, there will be good news for both of us.'

Maud took her companion's hand in a helpless, imploring way that went to Felicia's very heart; but, if her life had depended on it, no spoken word would come.

There are some things in life, some desperate chances, some horrible possibilities of suffering, which seem to strike one mute.

Maud seemed now to have come across some such crisis of existence. She followed Felicia about; they took the children for a walk; she went almost unconsciously about the littie routine of their home-life; all the time she seemed to herself in a sort of dreadful dream, but she turned faint and chill as the messengers now and again came clambering up the gorge, each with his fresh item of news from the world below, some one of them, as she knew must be the case, carrying with him the sentence of her fate.

'It makes my blood run cold,' she told Felicia afterwards, 'to see one of them coming even now.'

Sutton's words of farewell to her were not, however, destined to be his last. The next day a good friend at Government House sent them a copy of a telegram from head-quarters, which showed that Sutton's life was at any rate in no immediate danger. Then came a letter to Felicia from her husband. He had been up to head-quarters, he said, and stayed two days with Sutton. He was a good deal knocked about; there was a bullet lodged in his side, which had been troublesome, and he had been much bruised by his horse rolling across him. But there was no danger; in a week or two he would be able to move, and meanwhile he was in splendid air, and well looked after.

Then Maud went to her precious locket once again, and wept over it tears of joy, gratitude, and love. The mists had cleared away, the world was irradiated with happiness and hope; even the blackened hillside opposite had caught a ray of sunshine and seemed to smile back at her. She felt a very child again in the lightness of her heart; and Felicia, in a graver but not less happy mood, breathed a deep prayer of fervent gratitude that the calamity so near and terrible had passed away, leaving this young bright life as bright as ever.

CHAPTER XXV.

AN INVALID.

How do I love thee ?   Let me count the sums.
I love thee to depth and breadth and height
My soul can reach, when feeling out of sight
For the ends of Being and Ideal Grace.

WHEN, a month later, Sutton was carried into Dustypore he was, as anyone would have felt, a fit subject for romance, and Maud was just in the mood to appreciate all that was romantic about him to the full. She had been thinking about this event, and fancying it, and dreaming about it for weeks past, poor child, till it had become for her the very climax of existence. As the time for its realisation drew near she had been haunted by nervous apprehensions as to

whether she had not misinterpreted Sutton's
words of kindness at that last interview,
and whether the moment of disillusionment
might not be now arriving.   Sutton, so a
morbid mood suggested, might have meant
nothing ; or his words, perhaps, proved only
a passing tenderness, engendered by the
special circumstances of the hour.   Her
fancy, perhaps, had dressed up a few careless
expressions into something serious.   But
there came a truer voice which said that it
was not so ; that Sutton was not a man of
careless words or a transient mood, and that
a pledge had been given, though without
actual spoken vow, which he assuredly would
redeem on his return.   On the whole, then,
though not absolutely without a misgiving,
Maud was joyous and courageous, and her
heart was light within her. She, however,

felt herself becoming greatly embarrassed and excited as the hour of Sutton's arrival drew near ; the most needless blushes came flushing into her cheeks ; the simplest things seemed difficult to answer. Felicia knew, Maud was certain, pretty well how matters stood ; knew, at any rate, that there was something between her and Sutton : yet Maud had never summoned up courage to inform her what it was, nor had Felicia chosen to enquire. It was rather agitating, accordingly, that Felicia should now be about to have an opportunity of judging for herself how matters stood.

Then Sutton arrived, too suffering from his wound to be moved except in a doolie ; and was got, with a great deal of trouble and pain apparently, to the sofa in Vernon's study, which was turned into his sitting-room

for the time being, and where the invalid
was to spend the day. Here he lay, a close
prisoner, as feeble as a bad wound and a
month's fever could make him, and quite in
a condition for judicious nursing. A man in
such a plight wants company—pleasant,
gentle, noiseless, unexciting, feminine, if possible ; he wants to be read to, and sung and
played to ; he wants cooling drinks, which,
when mixed and administered by a hand
like Felicia's, are more than nectar ; he wants
those delicious idle gossips, for which the
healthy, busy side of life so seldom provides
either the opportunity or the mood. If a man
lack these, an illness is a dreary affair ; if he
has them, it may be amongst the pleasantest
hours of his life.

All these pleasant conditions now
attended the fortunate Sutton's convales-

cence. Felicia welcomed him with a joyful cordiality, and devoted herself with enthusiasm to the task of making his imprisonment as little wearisome as might be. Vernon stole an hour from his office to read him the 'Pall Mall Gazette ;' Maud found herself busy with the rest, a willing attendant on the happy warrior in his hour of weakness. Everybody made a great deal of him. Felicia's little girls, coming with much modesty and many blushes, brought him a nosegay apiece, and kissed his hand with a sort of affectionate reverence. His face was wan and thin, and marked with lines of suffering ; but the sweet, kind smile was still the same, and the honest eyes and finely-chiselled brow. On the whole Maud found him handsomer and ten times more touching than ever before. She knew, too, before they had been a minute in each other's company that all was well with her. The time of separation, uncertainty, distress, was done : happiness, greater than she had ever dreamed of, was already hers. Her foot stood already on the crowning ridge of existence, and all the horizon blazed with the golden clouds of Hope and Joy. ·

One effect that Sutton always had upon her she was especially conscious of just now : she had no feeling of shyness with him, such as she felt with all the world beside ; he stirred her being too profoundly for any slighter feeling to find a place. Shyness deals with the superficial, slighter outcomings of life.   Sutton seemed to transport her to another world of thought and feeling : thoughts too high and feelings too intense to heed the mode of their expression.   The consequence was that it seemed quite natural to Maud for her to be waiting on him ; and who had so good a right as she to that pleasant duty ?

Then presently Felicia went away with the children, and the two were again, for the first time, alone together.

'Come,' Sutton said, changing his manner instantly, 'sit down by me and tell me all that has happened since we parted on the mountain's side. You missed me a little, I hope ?'

'Yes,' said Maud, simply, looking at him with fearless, trusting eyes ; 'your going was the end of all our pleasure—we went away to the Gully, and then came your accident ·and some dreadful days of anxiety. Since then everything has seemed a sort of dream.'

'It has seemed a dream to me sometimes,' said Sutton, 'as I lay and wondered whether the happiness I fancied for myself was real or fable. Things befall one so suddenly in life, and strokes of good or ill fortune take one so by surprise, that one distrusts one's own belief about them; and cannot fancy that the old life which went before has been all transfigured. Now, however, I see you, and hear you, and have you about me, I begin to feel it was not a dream after all.'

'It was no dream,' said Maud, in her serious way; 'here is your locket, which I have been keeping for you since we parted.'

'No,' said the other, giving back the proffered locket, and keeping the hand which gave it in captivity. 'You shall keep it now, if you will, for good and all; that is, if you have a fancy for an old soldier, wounded and battered as you see me. Here I shall be for weeks, I suppose, a burden on the friends who are good-natured enough to be my nurses. You will have to tend me, as Elaine did Launcelot in his cave.'

' I will,' Maud said, wrapped into a mood which left her scarcely mistress of herself. ' My love is as great as hers was. I have been living all these weeks only that I might see you again. I must have died if you had not come back, or come back other than I hoped.'

The die was cast—the words were spoken ; they came out naturally, spontaneously, almost unconsciously, before Maud had time to know what she was about, or to judge of the wisdom and propriety of what she was saying. They were the truth ;

they were what she had been feeling and saying to herself for weeks past; they were the
true outcoming of her honest heart ; and yet
no sooner were they spoken than Maud felt
an awful conviction that they had better
have been left unsaid ; they were more, far
more, than anything which had been said
on Sutton's part to her.   Was it wrong, un-
womanly, indecorous, thus to have declared
herself and torn the veil from her feelings
without waiting for a lover's hand to remove
it ?   The thought was torture; the blood
came rushing to her cheeks and forehead ;
her very hand which Sutton was holding in
his own, emaciated and bloodless, was blushing too.   She could say nothing, she could
do nothing but stay, helpless, having made
her confession, and wait for Sutton to rescue
her.

As he lay there, holding her hand in his, clasping it with a firm, tender grasp, which seemed to be expressive of all she wanted, Felicia came into the room. Maud stood there, scarlet, and moved not, nor did Sutton seem inclined that she should.

'Felicia,' he said, 'you are the good angel of us both, and this moment would have been incomplete without you. Maud has just consented to become my wife.'

Felicia took Maud to her arms in a sort of rapture of happiness; her heart was too full for speech. It was a delightful relief from the anxiety and distress which had been weighing upon her all the summer, and which had of late grown into an acute pang. She felt grateful to both parties, who had at last brought about the result for which she had wished so anxiously, and of which she had somehow begun to despair.

Maud, on her part, felt it natural that Sutton should, at a trying emergency, have protected her skilfully, considerately, efficiently from the embarrassment into which her outspokenness had betrayed her; it was like himself to do so, and typical of the sort of feeling of confidence with which he always inspired her.   There was a delightful sense of safety and protection in being with him. How should her heart not beat high at the thought that this safety and protection would ever more be hers !

CHAPTER XXVI.

DESVŒUX IN DESPAIR.

All through love
Protested in a world of ways save one :
Hinting at marriage.

THE news of Maud's engagement was
naturally a congenial topic for gossip in
Dustypore. The romantic circumstances
under which it had come about, lent themselves readily to the superaddition of any
details, necessary, in the teller's opinion, in
order to bring the story to the correct pitch
of embellishment. Everybody considered
Maud a lucky girl ; some cynics remarked

G 2

that once again Sutton had shown himself
the most courageous of mankind ; and Mrs.
Vereker said, sentimentally, that she feared
poor Desvœux would *this time* be really
broken-hearted. There was some satire
lurking in the words 'this time,' because
the present occasion was by no means the
first on which the same sort of thing had
occurred. Desvœux was one of those inconveniently adjusted temperaments to which
no woman is completely delightful till she
has become unattainable. His relations to
the opposite sex did not as a general rule
appear to involve anything of a seriously
pathetic order ; but no sooner was a girl
engaged to some one else than he awoke
to the terrible discovery that he was deeply
in love with her himself, and deeply aggrieved by her betrothal to another. He was

known not to be a marrying man ; he made no secret of his dislike of matrimony as an institution ; still he greatly resented other people's marriages. Whenever any ladies of his acquaintance got married he used to send them the most lovely bridal presents, with beautiful little gilt-edged notes on the finest satin-paper, politely intimating that he was broken-hearted. Sometimes his feelings were too much for prose, and his melancholy would break out into epigrammatic versicles ; sometimes the gift bore only an inscription eloquent in its reticence—'*Le don d'un triste célibataire,*' or '*Avec un soupir.*' The presents, however, were so very pretty (for Desvœux's tastes were of the extravagant order), that their fair recipients, for the most part, took them, sighs, poetry, and all, without enquiring too rigidly into the giver's actual frame of mind. As most of the young ladies who had for some years past been married at Dustypore had experienced something of the sort, they probably compared notes, and reassured each other as to the probability of a disease, from which Desvœux had already more than once recovered, not proving fatal on any subsequent occasion.

Maud's engagement, however, touched Desvœux more nearly than any previous blows of the same description. Her joyous childish beauty, the readiness of her wit, the quickness of her replies, the great fun which they always had whenever Fortune was kind enough to throw them together; Maud's unconcealed appreciation of himself, despite the coquettish airs in which she now and then indulged; the ready frankness which invited intimacy so pleasantly—all had gone deep into Desvœux's heart, and he had grown to feel a sort of proprietorship in them, which it vexed him terribly to feel suddenly at an end. He felt certain that Maud liked him very much ; and certain, doubly certain, now, that he intensely admired her. No one else, he felt bitterly, had an equal right to do so. That Sutton, too, should be the fortunate rival made defeat all the bitterer. Sutton's good qualities were precisely those which Desvœux could least appreciate ; his military prowess did not impress him in the least ; his chivalry touched no corresponding chord ; his ideas of duty seemed pedantic, his feelings about women an anachronism.

If there was one thing in which it was especially irritating that such a man should

have carried the day, it was in the ascend-
ancy over ladies, which Desvaux considered
as his especial forte.   He piqued himself not
a little on his knowledge of the sex, his insight into their weaknesses, his experienced
tact in dealing with them to the best account.
He had established what he considered a
perfectly satisfactory footing with Maud, and
had spent no little time, trouble, and sentiment in the process.   It was a cruel humiliation to be rudely displaced from this agreeable eminence by a mere common-place
soldier, who had lived all his life in a camp,
and talked about women like a child.
Women are, Desvœux came bitterly to feel,
inscrutable, and the cleverest or stupidest of
mankind alike puppets in their hands, when
they have a passion to gratify or a secret to
conceal.   Anyhow, the news of Maud's en-

gagement set his heart a-beating, and sent his spirits down to zero. He was dining with the officers in the Fort when the an nouncement was made. One of them had been calling at the Vernons', and had heard the interesting fact from Felicia's own lips. ' Honneur aux braves ! ' cried Desvœux, with ostentatious merriment, tossing off his glass. ' Here's to their very good healths.' He was an adept at concealing his feelings, but a near observer might have seen that his hand trembled so that it was with difficulty he could carry his glass to his lips, and that, despite his jovial tones, he had turned deadly pale.

' I am glad she has come into the Army, at any rate,' said some one.

' Of course,' said Desvaux ; ' it is the old story. " J'aime beaucoup les militaires."

What chance have we poor civilians when a red jacket is in the field ?'

'And what, pray,' said one of the guests, a new arrival, ' is the lady's name ?'

Desvœux had risen from the table, and was moving towards the billiard-room. 'Her name,' he said, stopping in the act of lighting a cigar, 'is that of the rest of her sex—frailty.'

' Desvœux is hard hit this time,' observed one of a little knot who lingered behind the rest over their wine. ' He really loved her.'

'Fiddlededee!' said another. ' Desvœux love her, indeed !'

' He will have to drop all that now,' observed a third. 'Sutton would wring his neck for him or pitch him out of the window, if he as much as dared look at her !'

The fact, however, was that, conceal it as

he would, Desvœux was hard hit. His usual
expedient of buying a handsome wedding
present and writing the lady some poetry
quite broke down : Maud's bright eyes and
glowing cheeks, her beautiful upper lip, now
full of pretty scorn, now melting into a smile
that was sweetness itself, haunted him in his
dreams. He lit his pipe, he raged about
the room, he denounced the perfidy of
womankind, he read all the most horrible
passages in all the worst French novels in
his possession, he quoted all the fiercest cynicism of Chamfort and Rochefoucauld, in
vain, in vain ; there was Maud, enthroned
unquestioned mistress of his heart, and it was
labour lost to endeavour to displace her.

In course of time Desvœux lashed himself
into a most uncomfortable state of mind,
and became perfectly convinced that Maud

had treated him most cruelly. Accordingly, when next they met, his appearance was suggestive of a Byronic gloom of the very deepest dye; his handkerchief was tied with the negligence which spoke of shattered hopes, and his general demeanour was that of a man for whom the world was over. Maud was really in consternation at her friend's metamorphosis, and felt herself growing inconveniently shy. She was conscious of an instinctive apprehension that Desvœux was going to bring about a scene. His face of martyrdom was a study in the completeness of its woe.

'You expect me to wish you joy,' he said, 'and so I do. May all bright things attend you wherever you go, and wheresoever you are! The news of your engagement surprised and hurt me, of course.'

'Surprised and hurt you, Mr. Desvœux!' cried Maud, with increased alarm. 'I can't think why it should do that, or why you should look so very odd and—untidy.'

'Cannot you?' cried the other, stalking about the room, and fanning the flame of his excitement. 'I suppose not; you women are all so heartless.'

'No, we are not,' said Maud; 'and if we were, I do not see that you, of all people in the world, have any right to complain. Come, now, tell me what is the matter. Has the Agent been scolding you?'

'The Agent!' cried Desvœux, in tones of the profoundest disgust. 'You little traitress, don't you know as well as possible that there is only one thing in the world that could really hurt me, and that you have done it?'

'I!' exclaimed Maud, in horror. 'I'm sure I am very sorry. You must try and forget me.'

'Try and fly to the moon!' said Desvœux. 'I shall remember you all my life, to my cost, as the most bewitching little piece of mischief in existence. Why am I so unfortunate? I wish to goodness I had never seen you.'

'I am sure,' said Maud, fervently, 'I wish to goodness you never had, since it makes you so unhappy. But remember, if you please, that I had no idea of what you were feeling. You never told me, you know.'

'Who was to guess that Sutton would be so abominably precipitate? I thought he was safe with his soldiers and out of harm's way. Besides, told you! Why, you knew as well as possible that I adored you. Don't you remember how I squeezed your hand at the last Government House ball ? '

'And don't you remember,' cried Maud, indignantly, 'how I refused to dance a single round dance with you all the evening in consequence, and only gave you a Lancers to prevent your being laughed at ? '

'I only wish you could feel my heart beating,' said Desvœux, feeling that interesting organ, and apparently horrified at its activity.

'That is because you will go stamping about the room in that absurd way, instead of sitting still and talking quietly. Come, now, Mr. Desvœux, come and sit down and wish me joy kindly and pleasantly, or I never will speak to you again.'

'Little tyrant!' said the other, doing as he was bid as meekly as could be wished. 'And to think that you should be growing lovelier every day, and more charming, if possible, and all for Sutton! Speak to me, indeed! Why, you will not dare open your mouth for fear of a scandal.   Sutton will make you cut me, you will see, as an old admirer.'

'Indeed,' said Maud, upon whom Desvœux's flattery always told with some effect, 'I have not the slightest intention of giving up my old friends.   Why should I ?   Only you will not make love to me, of course.'

'Oh, of course not,' said the other, with a laugh.   'But tell me, now, are you not a wee bit sorry for a poor fellow who is breaking his heart about you ?'

'Breaking his fiddlestick!' cried Maud, bursting out laughing.   'Why, Mr. Desvœux, you don't, I assure you, know what you say.   It is very kind of you to like me, and admire me, and so forth, and I am very much obliged.'

'Don't, don't, for heaven's sake, talk like that,' cried the other. 'It is not kind of me at all to be over head and ears in love with you, but just my misfortune. But, tell me: they teased you into it, did they not?'

'Teased me into it!' cried Maud, tossing her head indignantly. 'How little you know!'

'Yes,' said the other, positively, 'it is obvious. You are an orphan—you have that sweet, interesting, dependent look that orphans have; and Mrs. Vernon made it up; set Sutton to flirt with you; everybody observed that much last summer; and then, no doubt, told you that you had been flirting and were bound to accept him. Why

didn't you pluck up heart of grace and say
" No ? " '

'Because I plucked up heart of grace to
say "Yes." Do you think that Colonel
Sutton is a sort of man who needs anyone
to help his wooing ? '

'I do,' said Desvœux, with provoking
persistency, ' and Mrs. Vernon gave him every
assistance. I only wish she would have
done half as much for me.'

'Well, then,' cried Maud, in a passion, 'if
you must know, it was I that proposed to
him—not he to me ; and I adore the tip of
his little finger more than all the other men
and women in the world. Now do you think
they teased me into it ? '

' No ; but if you begin with so much enthusiasm you will come to dislike him very
much before long. His little finger indeed !

And here am I left out in the cold! What am I to do?'

'Write and consult Mrs. Vereker,' said Maud. From which unfeeling remark it may be inferred that she believed less in Desvœux's broken-heartedness than he was inclined to do himself.

'Well,' said her companion, with a resigned air, which Maud felt had a touch of reproachful dignity in it, 'laugh at me as you will. I love you, and always shall.'

'Nonsense!' said Maud. 'Here comes my cousin. I have a great mind to tell her, and get her to comfort you.'

The interview was over. Maud had stuck to her programme, which was to treat Desvœux with an airy indifference, and his protestations with ostentatious disbelief. Nevertheless his words were not without effect. Had she been less inexperienced Maud would have known that she had allowed him to leave off in a most dangerous position ; that of an admirer whose homage was sufficiently congenial to be allowed a hearing, whom it was within her power to have at any moment at her feet, and who, whether rightly or wrongly, felt he had some show of right to be aggrieved and disappointed at her declared preference for another man.

There was another person, however, besides Desvœux to whom the news of Maud's engagement gave a serious shock.

One of Sutton's first acts, after Maud and he had mutually ascertained each other's views, was to scribble a line to Boldero, announcing the joyful event ; and he had done so, too full of his own happiness to pay much attention, even had he known more than he did, to the view his friend might take of it. All that he knew, however, was that Boldero, like all the world, was a great admirer of his future wife. This was but natural, and Sutton, without the least misgiving, accepted the position. 'My dear old boy,' he wrote, ' you will, I know, be pleased to hear a good piece of news of me, to make up for my bad luck the other day. Come over as soon as you can. and wish me joy. Meanwhile, remember, of course, that you must be my groomsman.'

' His groomsman !' Boldero sat, pale and speechless, and stunned by the sudden overthrow of all his hopes. The day-dream of his existence was ended by the stern awakening. Life—all that part of life, at least, which is worth living—was, he felt bitterly, over for

him.   It was, to use Heine's expressive
figure, as if some one had climbed up a
celestial ladder, rolled up the bright blue sky
and taken down the sun; only the dismal
scaffolding, the dust, the gloom remained.
Maud, though she had never quite en-
couraged him to hope, had never bidden him
despair, and figured, we may be certain, the
lovely chatelaine of all his castles in the air.
He found out now to his cost how full his
thoughts had been of her.   And now it was
all over.   His pleasant hope lay shattered on
the ground.   The blow was hard to bear;
none the easier, perhaps, that it was his
dearest friend's hand that struck it.

Being, however, a man of pluck and
determination, he sat down courageously,
wrote a cheery note of congratulation to the
fortunate winner of the prize, promised his

services as groomsman or anything else
which Sutton wished, and then ordered his
horse and rode twenty miles to an outlying
village, where there was a troublesome revenue dispute to be settled, which he had
had in his eye for weeks past as wanting a
visit from the Collector.

CHAPTER XXVII.

CHRISTMAS AT DUSTYPORE.

Truth is the strong thing. Let man's life be true—
And love's the truth of mine—time proves the rest.

CHRISTMAS had arrived, and Christmas was a
festival observed at Dustypore with all the
emphasis proper to men who had carried
their Lares and Penates beneath a foreign
sky, and were treasuring in alien regions the
sacred fire of the paternal hearth.

The weather was cold enough to realise
all that English tradition requires as 'season-
able' in the way of climate. For weeks past
great bullock-carts, piled high with gnarled
heaps of jungle-wood, had been creaking

along the dusty tracks from the outlying villages and supplying the Station with materials for Christmas-fires of appropriate magnificence. The air was deliciously clear, crisp, and invigorating : the searching wind came with its breath frozen from the Elysian snows, and left a hoary rime on all the country's face. English habits began to resume their sway : people were glad to forego the morning ride, and came down to breakfast at half-past nine with red noses and blue fingers, and, romantic reminiscence of European life, extremely bad colds in their heads.

Dustypore surrendered itself to holiday-making. The Salt Board suspended its sittings. The vehement Blunt, finding that no work was to be got out of anyone for love or money, started off into the country with his rifle, after black-buck and jungle-partridges. The courts were closed for a fortnight, and judges and collectors devoted themselves to sweeping off long arrears of morning calls. Contingents of visitors from all the surrounding out-stations came pouring in to share the festivities : every house was full and more than full; for, by the hospitable usages of India, when your spare-rooms are filled you order tents to be pitched in the garden, and enlarge your encampment as each new guest arrives. An Indian house is, therefore, viewed as to its capacities for hospitality, extremely elastic, and just now every house in Dustypore had its elasticity tested to the utmost. Felicia was renowned as a hostess; and there were half-a-dozen friends whose winter holiday would have lost half its charm if spent anywhere but beneath

her roof. There was a mixture of joyous-
ness and pathos in these Christmas gather-
ings which suited her temperament exactly,
and showed her in her sweetest, most at-
tractive mood. Her guests invariably went
away with cheered spirits and lightened
hearts, and a little store of remembered kindness to last them through the dreary months
to come. Nor was Felicia alone in her good
intentions. Everybody set about keeping
Christmas with heroic good-nature. The
Agent gave a ball in the state apartments in
the Fort. The Dustypore Hunt had a home
meet and a lunch. The 'Tent Club' organised a pig-sticking expedition for the
keener sportsmen. The Volunteers had a
gala-day, and were formed into a hollow
square, and panegyrised by the General of
the Division on their loyalty and discipline.

The Vernons gave some private theatricals, and Felicia and Maud made a great
success as Portia and Nerissa, in the 'Mer-
chant of Venice.' Desvœux, who was entrusted with the part of Shylock, heroically
shaved off his moustache, and transformed
himself into the most frightful of old Israel-
ites, with a hook-nose and beard of diabolical
aspect. The way in which he rolled his
eyes when Gratiano exclaimed, 'Now, in-
fidel, I have thee on the hip!' had twice
caused Maud to explode in irrepressible
laughter at rehearsals, and very nearly
caused a break-down among the actors at
the final performance. Altogether it was
very like home, and very pleasant, as all
the party felt.

These Indian festivities are, perhaps,
none the less festive, and certainly the more

touching, for the fact that at least half the holiday-makers have a dark, sad corner in their hearts which has to be hidden from the world's eye, and to be ignored in the common intercourse of life. Separation is the dark cloud which hangs over an Indian existence : husbands and wives, mothers and children, forced asunder, perhaps at the very time when union is most delightful : and living (how maimed and sad a life !) in the absence of all that is best-beloved. They put a brave face upon it, but the heartache is there all the same. What a strong pulse of love and tenderness and sorrow goes throbbing week by week across half the world from the wives and children at home to the lonely exile, struggling bravely with his fate in the far-off Indian station—what dear, ill-spelt, round-hand, stupid letters, which yet are wept over with such passionate pleasure, and treasured with such pious care ! People have a cheap tariff for telegraphing back to India their safe arrival in England, with a rupee extra for saying that the traveller 'is better.' What a story it tells of anxious men in India toiling over work, with their hearts far away with the shattered, invalid lady, or flickering child's life, carried away to cool regions in hopes of saving it !

Take, for instance, little Major Storks, who was stage-manager for the Vernons' theatricals, and sang a comic song between the acts. He is a grizzly, wizen, well-tanned, wiry little fellow, but has, under that rough exterior, as brave and tender a heart as ever beat. He is in charge of the Rumble Chunder Canal, and bestows on it all a lover's assiduity : for it he thinks, he writes, he plans, he labours early and late ; he rides about in the most demented fashion until the sun has dried him up into a perfect mummy. He knows the Canal's ways and manners— how much water it ought to pour per second ; how much it *does* pour ; which of the bridges are infirm ; where the silt is accumulating ; where the water is being wasted or stolen. He drives his subordinates frantic by a zeal in which they cannot participate and a thoroughness which they cannot shirk. To the world outside he seems the merest drudge. To-day, however, he is in paradise. It is Christmas morning, and the mail has brought him a goodly budget of letters, all redolent of home and tender conjugal love, and, precious alleviation of exile, photographs of half-a-dozen little Storks. He sits now, with all his

family before him, with tears of joyful satisfaction in his eyes. What comely lads!
what sweet, ingenuous little girls! what dear,
familiar looks, the legacy of a youth that has
passed away, greeting him from every little
portrait! In a moment Storks' soul quits its
shabby tenement of clay and its hot sur-
roundings, and is away in England with wife
and children; the wife, whose heart has
ached for many a dreary year of separation;
the children, who have been taught to love
him with a sort of romantic piety, all the
more for being far away; the pleasant, cool,
idle life in England, which lies afar off, a sort
of Promised Land, if ever his long, rough task
in India can get itself performed. Then, in
the fulness of his heart, he will put on his
shabby uniform and order round his shabby
dogcart, and go and show his treasures to

Felicia, who will, he knows, have a quick
sympathy for his pleasure and his pain; and
when the two act in a charade that night
each will know that all is not as merry as it
seems, but that, under a stoical calmness,
lie thoughts and hopes and pangs which stir
the very depths of a man's being, and which
require all the help that sympathy and kind-
liness can give.

The last and most interesting occasion of
the holidays was one in which Sutton and
Maud played a leading part. Sutton had
a two months' inspection march before him,
and no better sort of honeymoon could
be desired. The country through which
they were to go was wild but very picturesque. Sutton's duties would never take
him away for more than a few hours; and
camp life is idyllic in its freedom, uncon-

straint, and tranquillity. Existence has something charming about it when each morning's ride takes you through new scenes to a new home, in which you live as comfortably for the next twenty-four hours as if you had been there all your life. Maud was in rapture at the prospect, nor was her happiness lessened by the arrival of the most perfect Arab to be found in Bombay—her husband's wedding gift to her—on which her long journey was to be performed. To Sutton these weeks seemed the fitting threshold of the new and brighter existence into which he was about to pass. Each day Maud bound herself closer to his heart by some sweet act or word, some unstudied outpouring of devotion, childish in its simplicity and unconsciousness, but womanly in its serious strength : some sympathetic note which vibrated harmoniously to his inmost soul. 'To be with you, dear,' he said, 'is like travelling through a lovely mountain country, where each turn in the road opens up a fresh delight—you charm me in some new fashion every hour.'

To this sort of remark Maud had no need of any other reply than that easiest and most natural of all to feminine lips, which dispenses with the necessity of spoken words. Her kisses were, we may be certain, eloquent enough to Sutton's heart, irradiated for the first time with a woman's love, and beating high with a courageous joyfulness and hope.

By the end of January Sutton was well enough to be emancipated from the pleasant thraldom of an invalid's sofa ; nor could his march be any longer delayed. One afternoon, accordingly, the little world of

Dustypore assembled to see the brave soldier and the beautiful girl made man and wife. Boldero came in from the District and performed his part as groomsman with creditable stoicism. No one—Maud and Sutton least of all—had the least idea that he was assisting at the sacrifice of all his hopes.

Desvœux preserved his tragic demeanour to the last, presented Maud with a diamond pendant which must have gone far into his quarter's income, and refused obstinately to return thanks for the bridesmaids—a task which was traditionally assigned to him in Dustypore, and which, on all ordinary occasions, he accepted with alacrity and performed with success.

CHAPTER XXVIII.

MORNING CLOUDS.

——The little rift within the lute.

Sutton brought back his bride in April, all the better, as it appeared, in health and spirits for her two months' expedition. The beautiful rose of her cheeks had a tinge of brown which spoke only of healthy exercise in the open air. Everybody pronounced her prettier, brighter, and more charming than ever. She was in the highest spirits to be back, and Sutton seemed pleased to bring her, and to be once more amongst old friends.

To all who saw them, except Felicia's

observant eye, they seemed everything which
a newly-wedded pair should wish to be.
But Felicia felt less confident of their happiness. Whether Maud's letters had unconsciously sounded a little note of distress, or
whether it was that she knew both their
natures so well, and how they ought to
harmonise, that the least approach to discord
caught her ear, something, at any rate, made
her aware of the existence of a subtle dis-
quietude between Maud and her husband.
The discovery, or rather the suspicion, filled
her with a distress which she attempted in
vain to ignore. She found herself joining
languidly and insincerely in the chorus of
gratulation which the Dustypore community
set up over the happy couple. When Mrs.
Vereker came to call, rustling in the love-
liest of new dresses, and poured out a little

stream of gossiping remarks—how pretty it was to see them together, and what a charming lover Sutton made—and was not Maud a picture of a girl-wife ?—Felicia responded with a coldness which puzzled her visitor, and which Felicia was conscious of trying in vain to conceal. Something, her fine instinct told her, was amiss. One alarming symptom was the obvious relief which Maud found in her society, and the profuse tenderness and affection which she displayed whenever there was no one else to see. She lavished on her a sort of unconscious fondness, for which Felicia looked in vain in her behaviour to her husband; with him her affection seemed constrained, conscious, too deferential to be natural and happy. There was about Maud, when she and Felicia were alone together, a joyous self-abandonment to animal high spirits, which was for ever flowing out into some pretty childish act of fun or affection, but which vanished at the appearance of Sutton or any other onlooker. She became a girl again—she sang, she danced, she got into the wildest games with the children—she let off her excitement and mirth in a thousand natural acts. Then Jem would come in, and it all seemed to die away. When visitors arrived, and Felicia had presently more on her hands than was at all to her taste, Maud would seem to enjoy it, and to get amused and interested; then, as the door closed upon the strangers, she would come and throw her arms round Felicia and caress her, as if her one feeling about the visit was that it had been an inconvenient restraint on love which was wanting every moment to express itself in some outspoken fashion. 'I love you the best, the best of all,' she would say, impetuously.

'Of all women,' Felicia put in.

'Of all women and of all men too, except Jem,' Maud answered. 'Yes, and I believe I love you better even than Jem ; anyhow I love you.'

More than once, too, Felicia detected little manœuvres on Maud's part to walk or drive with her, and to quit her husband's society in order to do so. Altogether Felicia felt frightened, anxious, and sad about her friends ; and Vernon, who always knew her melancholy moods, and could generally guess their cause, in vain endeavoured to console her with the assurance that all was right, and that Sutton's had been a wise and happy choice. The truth was that the march had not been altogether a success. A great

authority on such matters has said that
people often endanger the permanent happiness of married life by putting too severe a
strain upon it at its outset. Now, a two
months *tête-à-tête* is a serious strain. Life
wants something besides mere affection to
make it run smoothly : it wants the ease and
comfort of familiarity, the freedom of tastes
ascertained to be congenial, the pleasant
usages of common action. The first year of
wedded life is, no doubt, a series of experi-
ments in getting on; two wheels, however
nicely fitted, are likely to rub a little at
some point of contact or other. And then
paradise itself would lose its charm if it
were all the same ; and the days on Maud's
first journey had a distracting resemblance.
Her eyes ached with the interminable horizon
of dust and sand, the scrubby brushwood,

the lonely crumbling tomb, the rare clumps of palms, the scuffling bellowing herds of cattle. Sutton's cook, whom his master, in his simple tastes, believed a prodigy of culinary skill, used to send up the same dishes with depressing monotony, and, do what she would, Maud could not like them. Then some marches were over terribly rough ground, and her Arab made stumbles that took her breath away, though she was ashamed to say so. But it was not the little things which really mattered. Her husband's very nobility of nature oppressed her. A hundred times she had felt how good he was, how true, how really great, how chivalrous in his devotion, how tenderly considerate, and yet—and yet—something more unheroic would perhaps have been sometimes a relief. When the most ineffably stupid young officers rode across from some neighbouring station and plunged with cheerful volubility into the gossip of last season at Elysium, there was, Maud felt, something welcome in the humbler companion and the more trivial theme. Then, too, the solitary days oppressed her. Sutton had often outlying posts to visit, and would accomplish them by starting off three or four hours before Maud was awake, and making a *détour*, so as to meet her at their new halting-place at breakfast. On these mornings Maud had the company of an escort of troopers, her greyhound Punch, and her own thoughts, which were apt to get gloomy. Even Punch, she fancied, thought it a bore, and went along in a dejected fashion. Sometimes Sutton's work could not be so quickly disposed of, and he would be detained till the evening, and then the

solitary day seemed sad and interminably
long. More than once the tears had come
unbidden to her eyes. Did Sutton forget
her? Never for an instant, her heart told
her clearly enough ; but he did not perhaps
sufficiently realise the wants and wishes, the
flickering, uncertain spirits, the wayward
moods, the causeless melancholy of one who,
though invested with the dignities of womanhood, was in character and powers in reality,
still a child.

Then, though Sutton was never in the
slightest degree imperative, and though his
every spoken wish was law, Maud was
conscious sometimes of being kept in better
order than she liked, and being forced up to
a standard which was inconveniently high.
Her husband spoke little of his tastes ; no
word from him ever assumed the resem-

blance of a command, yet Maud not un-
frequently felt that a secret pressure was con-
straining her to something that was not
exactly congenial; she felt with an almost
distressing distinctness what her husband
liked and disliked, and the knowledge was
something of a burden.   She was conscious
when she hurt him : sometimes from mere
waywardness she chose to do it, but she hurt
herself in the process as much as him.   She
had given him her heart and made him all
her world, and was glad to have done so.
None the less there was sometimes an undefined pang about her self-devotion ; she became   restless,   anxious,   uncertain   in   her
moods, and the tears seemed to lie near the
surface, and would spring to light, in unwary
moments, at trifles too slight to cause their
flow.

Then on some matters her husband's tastes and hers were by no means in harmony. On one occasion Desvœux seized the opportunity of the Agent's camp being in the neighbourhood, and had ridden across and travelled a couple of marches with them. Maud had looked forward to seeing him with pleasure, and greeted his arrival with marked animation. The visit turned out as pleasant as she had expected, but the pleasure was marred by a secret conviction of her husband's disapproval. Nothing could quench Desvœux's light-heartedness or impede the easy flow of his amusing small-talk. Sutton, however, did not seem to find it amusing, and assumed, quite unconsciously, a dignified air, which Maud felt to be rather awful, though Desvœux seemed imperturbable. His spirits, however, were better, and she was more at her ease to be infected by them when Sutton was not by. It vexed her to the heart to know that it was so, but so she knew it was.

The morning that Desvœux went away was one of Sutton's busy days, and Maud was alone when their guest bade her farewell. ' Goodbye,' Maud said, with a sort of sigh. ' How I wish you could have stopped and ridden with me this morning! I shall be alone all day.' Was she smiling or crying, and did she really want his company; and was she neglected and miserable ?

Desvœux had galloped away with his heart in a tumult from queries such as these, cursing the cruel fate which obliged him to be at his master's camp, full thirty miles away, with endless boxes of despatches ready for disposal before to-morrow morning.

Thus it was that Maud's early married
life had not been without its morning clouds
and sorrows. Then, as people do when
they are unhappy, casting about for a cause
of her unhappiness, she began to reproach
herself. The old doubts of her fitness, her
worthiness for her position, her power to
retain her husband's love, began to haunt
her. 'Ah me!' she sometimes felt inclined
to cry, 'I fear that I am no true wife.' And
yet she knew that, not even if her inmost
thoughts were read, could she bring any
charge of doubtful love or allegiance against
herself. Sutton's men had, she had often
heard, begun to worship him when his
exploits in the Mutiny had raised their enthusiasm to its height. Maud felt that she
could understand the feeling ; in fact, she did

worship him with all her being. But then worship is not all that is wanted for a happy married life. Maud, at any rate, felt it delightful to be with Felicia once again.

CHAPTER XXIX.

THE HILL CAMP.

In the afternoon they came unto a land
In which it always seemèd afternoon.
All round the coast the languid air did swoon.

MAUD soon lost sight of her troubled spirits
in Felicia's society. Her doubts about her •
happiness in married life began to die away.
Her devotion to Felicia was a sentiment
which her husband thoroughly understood
and cordially approved.

' I used to be finely jealous of her, Jem, I
can tell you, in old days,' Maud would say to
him, 'and to think you liked her twenty
times better than some one else ; and indeed
I am not sure that I am not jealous now ;

only I am so much in love with her myself that I do not feel it.'

'Jealous!' Sutton would plead, 'Felicia is like a sister to me. It was she, I believe, who first hit out the brilliant idea of our being married.'

'Was it?' said Maud, blushing. 'I fancied that happy thought had been mine own. Well, Jem, if you never flirt with any one but her I will forgive you, because in my opinion she is an angel.'

The pleasant visit ended. Sutton had to go off to his camp, a hill station some three thousand feet above the sea, and therefore, as its enemies declared, combining all the drawbacks of hill and plain. Here they were to stay till June, when Sutton was to have his leave, and to take his bride up to Elysium for the rest of the summer. Even this prospect had not enabled Maud to bear the parting from her friend with equanimity. ' I wish—I wish,' she had said, wistfully, with the tears in her eyes—' what do I wish ? If only, dear Felicia, I could never go away from you!' Felicia bade her farewell with an aching heart, and some dark misgivings. They were not to meet at Elysium, for this year she had determined to establish her children at the ' Gully,' a little mountain abode, which Vernon had purchased some years before, and to divide her time between them and her husband till he could come up and join them. Then they had resolved to take a little march into the interior, where Felicia might get some new sketches and enlarge her stocks of ferns ; while Vernon might have a few days' shooting, unharassed by official cares and correspondence.

The Hill Camp proved a fearful place ;
worse, far worse, than anything on the
march. It was only to be endured till June,
happily, but still it looked terrific. The long
lines of huts, the horrible little abodes which
were honoured by the title of Officers'
Quarters ; the gaunt, hideous, treeless hills ;
the valleys blazing and withered, the dry
scene uncheered by a single streamlet ; the
dusty plateau, where the soldiers were
eternally marching, galloping, cannonading—
all the outer world seemed dull, parched,
repulsive. There was no other lady in the
camp but one, the surgeon's wife, large and
dark and hot, and, as Maud felt, horribly
realising one's ideas of an ogress. This
lady used to come and see her, and sit
gossiping and questioning, and telling long
stories, and shaking a great bird of paradise

feather in her head, till she made Maud's life a burthen to her. Then, after about three of these visitations, which Maud imagined that she had endured with angelic sweetness, the lady, for some inscrutable cause, took offence, and when next they met out of doors flung up her head, brandished the bird of paradise feather in the most menacing and defiant manner, and had evidently proclaimed a social war of an altogether implacable order.

'Oh, Jem! what *have* I done?' said Maud, with a shudder, as she passed.

'Something unforgivable, evidently,' said Sutton. 'We must make peace at once, because Surgeon Crummins could poison us all, if he pleased, next time we happen to be poorly. Let us have them to dinner.'

So the irascible lady and the surgeon

had to be asked to dinner; and dull and stiff and wearisome the dinner proved, and Maud's heart sank within her at the thought that these were to be her companions, and this the sort of life upon which she was embarked. She loved her husband, but what a price her love had cost her !

Flashes of brightness, however, break in upon the dreariest lot, and one cheering feature of this period was the arrival of a most interesting box from England, containing a highly important supplement to Maud's original *trousseau.* To take an array of pretty garments for a march of two months in the jungle had been out of the question, so that Felicia had determined that all Maud's dresses for the coming summer should not arrive till the time approached when they would be of use. In May, accordingly, there came two splendid cases, whose appearance announced the importance of their contents. Jem professed himself quite as excited as Maud, and set to work at once with chisel and hammer to disinter the treasures. There is something very delightful in such unpackings—far from home— the very air within seems English. The silver-paper has a charming familiar look; then each package as it comes out and is revealed excites a pleasing pang of excitement—and these boxes were mines of treasures. There were lovely ball-dresses, lying fresh, unruffled, ethereal as when they left the artist's hand; and a new habit, which made Maud feel how shabby hers had grown in her long tour; and a most charming morning dress, looped up into all sorts of fantastic costumes, which her prophetic soul told her would look very effective on the lawn at Government House ; and there were hats and bonnets, and flowers for the hair, culled surely by some fairy hand ; and amongst the other treasures was a fine pearl necklace, which old Mrs. Sutton had guarded for many a year for this especial end, and had re-set, and now sent, with all sorts of fond wishes and blessings, to her dear son's bride.

Sutton insisted on Maud's trying every-thing on ; and Maud, nothing loth, obeyed.

' Let us send across for Mrs. Crummins,' suggested her husband. ' If this will not appease her she is a fury.'

Accordingly, Maud wrote a little note, in great excitement :—' Dear Mrs. Crummins, *would* you like to see my new dresses, which have just arrived ? ' Mrs. Crummins *would* like it, of all things, and came across in about two minutes, under a big umbrella, bird of paradise and all, and was quite as much pleased as Maud, and plunged with her at once into mysteries of detail in which Sutton's male mind was incapable of sympathising. She heaved great sighs of wonder, delight, and satisfaction as each new treasure came to light, and ended by losing her heart and kissing Maud quite affectionately in her enthusiasm. 'Indeed they are very pretty, and so are you, my dear, and, as the Surgeon says, quite a refreshing sight for weary eyes.'

So Maud, who was ever ready for a proclamation of amity, signed peace at once, and before the week was out she and her new friend were on terms of the utmost confidence, and had arranged the bird of paradise in the very latest fashion, as shown in Maud's own hats, so that it really looked lovely. The result, however, of all this was, that Maud anticipated Elysium with greater glee than ever. A pearl necklace, a beautiful satin dress, a Paris fan, with lovely Watteau ladies gliding all about it—well, it was something to go from day to day and look at these treasures, but the moment for fruition had not arrived. They would have been quite thrown away on Sutton's troopers and mule-men, amid the horses and the dust.

Maud's grey habit, plaid dress, and broad pith hat was the only costume that would not have been ridiculous for the camp. No, the hour for real enjoyment had not arrived, and patience, as Maud had frequently occasion to observe, is a virtue easy to preach, but hard to practise, when the present is dull and the expected future a blaze of pleasure.

Then other things had occurred to intensify her anticipation of enjoyment at Elysium and her wish to go there. Mrs. Vereker had written her a letter which set her heart beating. ' The Governor-General and I,' that excellent lady wrote, ' have both arrived, and so the Season may be said to have begun. Our friends of the Twentieth are here in force, and are going to do wonders in the way of entertainment—everybody says it is to be *dazzling*. General Beau is here, as adoring as ever. The truth is, my rose bonnet is rather adorable, so, at least, *mes amis* inform me. By the way, that naughty Mr. Desvœux goes on as absurdly as ever about " some one," and declares quite seriously that he is broken-hearted.

'Silly fellow!' said Maud, and yet it rather pleased her.

'Can you dance a minuet?' the letter went on. 'We are all having lessons. There is to be one at Government House. General Beau's shrugs and shakes over it are delicious. Everybody declares that I do it to perfection—but everybody won't say so when "somebody" arrives and carries all before her. So you see, my dear, I make hay while the sun shines, and am not a bit jealous; but come and eclipse me as soon as you please, for I, too, rather love you.'

Two hot, dusty, weary months had still to pass. Over that dull interval Maud's imagination travelled, each day with lighter steps, to a paradise of excitement and delight.

CHAPTER XXX.

TEMPTATION.

We fell out, my wife and I,
And kiss'd again with tears.

SUCH being the state of things at Elysium, and such the state of Maud's feelings at the camp, imagine her dismay when Sutton came into the room one morning, with a letter in his hand, and a very vexed expression on his face, and said : ' Is not this a bore, Maud ? Here is a letter from the Chief telling me to go and inspect and report on all the suspected villages at once, and say what force we want. So we cannot go to Elysium after all.'

' Not go to Elysium ! ' cried Maud, flushing red, and the tears gathering to her eyes
before she had time to check them.   It
seemed to her, poor child, the very climax of
disappointment.

Her husband kissed her kindly.   ' I did
not know, dear,' he said, ' that you would
care about it so much.   I am such an old
salamander myself that I forget that other
people don't enjoy being grilled as much as
I do.   But what can be done ?   These
scoundrels—bad luck to them—must be reported on, and I must get the report
finished before my autumn march begins.'

' It cannot be helped, I suppose,' said
Maud, in a tone of despair, and retreating
gloomily to her bedroom ; for the tears kept
coming fast, and the news seemed worse and
worse each time she realised its import

afresh. No Elysium ! No holiday — no change — no charming balls — no beautiful dresses—no pleasant rides—none of the nice scenes on which her fancy had dwelt, the prospect of which had cheered her through the long, dull spring—no bright companions, full of mirth and flattery and devotion to herself ! Alas ! alas ! Maud felt that her trouble was too great to bear. Sutton followed her presently, in a great state of perturbation at her display of disappointment.

'Come, Maud,' he said, kindly, ' cheer up. You shall go and see Felicia if you like.'

But, alas ! Maud's tears had got the mastery of her. A long-pent-up stream of melancholy had burst, and nothing could stop it. She was inconsolable ; the disappointment, in itself a great one, had found her not too well prepared to bear it.   She wept, and would not, or could not, be comforted.

Sutton was completely disconcerted : to see her in trouble, and not be able to relieve it, wishing for anything that he could not give, grieving in this sort of hopeless fashion about what was to him scarcely more than an annoyance, was a new experience, and one which he was unprepared to meet. The fact was, though he did not know it, that Maud had got her head full of nonsense about Elysium.   Distance lent enchantment to the view, especially when the view was taken from the dusty, stupid camp.   Mrs. Vereker's foolish letter seemed bright and alluring : Desvœux's merry talk and romantic protestations, how full of amusement, interest, excitement it all seemed !   How unbearably dull in contrast the life about her !

Sutton often absent, often tired and silent, sometimes sad; never, Maud told herself, anything like amusing. Yes, it was too vexatious for all the heroism she could bring to bear upon it : her philosophy broke down.

' I know it is a hard life here,' said her husband, in vain attempts at consolation : ' it is hot and dull for you. I like it, but then I am used to it. But what can I do ? If only `Felicia were at Elysium you might go up to her.'

' There is Mrs. Vereker,' said Maud, suggestively.

' Mrs. Vereker !' exclaimed Sutton, in consternation. ' You surely——'

' She wrote very kindly the other day,' Maud said, cutting short her husband's protestation, ' and asked me to stay with her in her cottage.'

'But, Maud, you would not really like to go to her, would you?'

'I should not like to go,' Maud said, 'if you disapproved.'

'And I,' answered Sutton, suddenly nettled, 'would not have you stay unless you liked. How shall we decide?'

'You must decide,' said his wife, too much excited and too anxious to know well what she was about.

'Very well,' said Sutton, kindly, but with a sad tone that haunted Maud in after-times, 'I will decide. You shall go.'

Maud knew the tone in which he spoke as well as spoken words. She knew the look when he was hurt; she had watched it before. It told her now that she had never wounded him so deeply as to-day. Her heart smote her. He had hardly gone before she longed to repent and stay; and yet she could not make up her mind to the sacrifice which it would cost her. She had been reckoning so upon it that it seemed like the blotting out of all the brightness of her life. The prospect of the dreary, lonely summer was too grievous. So her heart went swaying to and fro: she grew more and more unhappy. Sutton was doubly kind and tender to her, and his look smote her to the heart. At last her good angel carried the day. ' Jem,' she said, ' I want to change my mind, please. I was mad just now, and do not know what possessed me. I do not want to go to Elysium or anywhere, if you cannot go with me. I am frightened at the idea of it, even at this distance. I am sure I should be wretched. You must forgive me, and forget my foolish tears.'

These two had perhaps never loved each
other quite so much as at this moment, nor
Maud been ever quite so loveable. She was
in her sweetest mood ; she wore a bright,
serene air which spoke of an unworthy
temptation overcome, a higher happiness
attained, a victory over her weaker, baser
self. Already, as happens in such cases,
it seemed to her incredible that she could
have wished for the lower pleasure which
had so nearly won her. As for Sutton, the
world was suddenly reillumined to him ; the
gloomy, terrible, agonising eclipse had passed:
all was sunshine and joy. His face showed
what he was feeling. He drew Maud to
him and kissed her with a serious, fervent
air, as if it were an act of worship ; he held
her as if it were impossible to him ever to
let her go. Maud knew that his iron frame

was shaken with vehement emotion; she saw a kind of rapture in his eyes, and read in them that she was well-beloved.

'Dear Maud,' he said, 'I should be wretched, the most miserable wretch alive, if ever any shade of doubt or coldness came between us two. You hold my life, dear, in your hand : my heart is wholly yours, and has no other life. If ever your love to me waned it would be death to me.'

And Maud, as she looked and listened, knew that it would.

'It can never wane, dear Jem,' she said, infected with her husband's mood, and clinging to him, as was her wont, like a child that needs protection. 'Every day you bind me closer to you ; only I fear—and ten times more after being such a goose as I was just now—that I am not half worthy of all you are to me.'

CHAPTER XXXI.

BOLDERO ON GUARD.

> Oh ! never work
> Like this was done for work's ignoble sake.
> It must have finer aims to spur it on!

THUS Maud and her husband were more than reconciled. Maud packed up her dresses, with a few natural sighs that so much sweetness should waste itself unseen, and set about passing the summer with heroical cheerfulness. Things took a turn for the better. A few thunder-storms had come to cool the world, and the early rains were covering the barren mountains with verdure, and bringing new life to Maud's garden. Mrs. Crummins was giving her lessons in water-colours, and altogether existence was less intolerable than she had believed it possible that it should be. Perhaps the momentary breach, followed so quickly by so thorough a reconciliation, had engendered an especial sweetness in her intercourse with her husband. Be that as it may, Maud had resigned Elysium, and settled down courageously to her home life, not, perhaps, without regret, but, at any rate, without discontent.

Before, however, their reconciliation had time to take effect in any alteration of their plans, events occurred which gave their thoughts a wholly new direction, and effectually settled for them what they were to do. Occasional cases of cholera, seeds sown by the scattered atoms of the great Fair the year before, had been occurring in various districts all through the winter, and at the first blush of spring the disease showed symptoms of breaking out in force. Week by week the 'Gazette' chronicled a marked diminution in other forms of sickness, an equally distinct increase in this. The doctors had a busy time in making preparations, and great were the cleansings, the whitewashings, the emptyings, the fillings-up, in many an immund old town and ill-odoured village, where the kingdom of Dirt had prevailed in unbroken tranquillity for generations past.

Outside each city a cholera camp was formed, with a view to the isolation of the sufferers. The District officers were at work from morning to night. The natives took it all with that slightly wondering acquiescence which is the normal attitude of mind

produced by the proceedings of the 'Sahib.'
It was the order of God that cholera should
come; it was likewise the order of the
'Sirkar' that houses should be whitewashed,
cesspools cleared out, and chlorodyne administered gratis to all who liked it; both
visitations were inscrutable, and to be endured with philosophic calm. The English
Doctor however, was, so ran the orthodox
belief, a dangerous fellow, and the old
'Hakún,' with his traditional nostrums,
no doubt the proper person to be killed or
cured by. The right thing, therefore, if one
became ill, was carefully to conceal the fact,
have surreptitious interviews with the native
physician, and, if die one must, be returned
as having died of some disease which would
not involve a visit from the 'Inspector
Sahib,' a conflagration of bedsteads and

clothes, a general effusion of whitewash, and consequent topsy-turveying of all the household. English doctors and native doctors, however, were of much the same avail, for King Cholera has as yet defied science to read his deadly mystery, and learn the secret of his rule. All that science can achieve is to narrow the limits of his ravages.

May had scarcely begun when two cases occurred in the Hill Camp, and Sutton, for the first time in his life, knew what it was to be afraid. He had given 'hostages to Fortune,' and death and danger for the first time looked really terrible when it was Maud who had to confront them. Fifty times Sutton cursed his folly and selfishness in not having sent her off earlier to the hills, out of harm's way.

While he was harassing himself with

vain regrets and self-reproaches, and puzzling his brains as to how the mistake might be even yet repaired, Maud herself added a new item to his perplexities by becoming decidedly unwell. She awoke unrefreshed and wretched ; declined the great treat of the day, her morning ride ; came shivering and appetiteless to breakfast, and confessed to feeling completely miserable. Her husband, the moment that he felt her dry, burning hand, exclaimed that she had got fever, gave her a welcome prescription to go back at once to bed, and sent off for the Doctor.

The reader of these pages, who knows the Sandy Tracts, would think that I did them scarcely justice if I omitted from the picture all reference to a visitation which to many of them formed, too often, a main feature of Indian existence. There is a Fiend

there, be it known, that comes, no one can
tell whence—from earth or air, or marshy
pool or frosty sky, or blazing sunny morning. However, when he comes he speedily
makes his arrival known to the guests whom
he favours with a visit. He shakes them
and racks them, and gets into their heads
and beats a kettledrum there; and sets a
tribe of imps to dance a sort of infernal
ballet all about each quivering limb; he
freezes them, so that the poor shivering
wretches bury themselves under mountains of
rugs and blankets, and go on shivering still;
he parches them till they feel like Dives in
torture; he turns their brains to mud, their
thoughts to chaos, their high spirits to the
very blackest gall. Most people, it is believed, when the demon first possesses them,
signalise his accession by a hearty cry; and

well they may, for among the other cheering thoughts which suggest themselves at the moment, one is that every time you have fever the likelier you are to have it yet again ; and that your way to recovery lies through a remedy which for bitterness and bewilderment is only not as bad as the disease for which it is invoked—quinine. In the Sandy Tracts they serve it to you hot, out of a black bottle, stopped with a twisted coil of paper, and heated half to boiling by being carried through the sun. It is at such a moment that existence naturally wears a sombre look, and that the Indian exile curses the ambition or the ill-luck that bore him to such a fortune beneath an alien sky.

Maud, however, was so far fortunate that she had the best and tenderest nurses that could be wished. The surgeon, delighted with so interesting a patient, was assiduous, considerate, and suggestive. Mrs. Crummins was more than a mother, and Sutton suddenly discovered a perfect genius for the science of an invalid's room. When Maud, after a week or two, began to get strong again there was no doubt in the little conclave that she ought to go to the hills. A great deal of illness was about—the cholera had been really serious—the fierce summer was coming quickly on—in another fortnight the journey would be almost impossible for all but the strongest. So it was settled for her to go ; and Sutton became very impatient and uneasy till she was safely off. Circumstances seemed to settle whither she should go. There had come the kindest letter from Mrs. Vereker, the moment she had heard of Maud's attack. Indian people are, it must be said for them, delightfully hospitable, and offer one bed and board for as long as one likes as a matter of course. ' Let me know the day, and I will send out my pony for the last stage in ; and I shall take the children into my room, which they will think great fun, and turn the nursery into a bedroom for my pretty invalid. Come, dear Maud, and I will promise you back your blooming cheeks in a fortnight!'

Sutton was touched by the kindness of a person to whom he had never been in the least polite ; and, in far too great a fright to be particular, or allow objections which would have suggested themselves at another time, he lost no time in writing to Boldero about the carriage to Elysium (for, without a little pressure in the matter of bullocks and camels from the District officer, carriage in the

Sandy Tracts is hard to find) ; and Boldero had written to say that happily he himself was going up on business, and would put his camp at Mrs. Sutton's disposal.

Accordingly Maud went up to the Hills in the utmost comfort, and with what would have struck European eyes as somewhat unnecessary pomp. The wild country in which they lived rendered an escort of cavalry an almost necessary feature of any but the shortest expedition, and she was quite accustomed to go out for her ride, in her husband's absence, attended by a couple of wild Sowars, whose rude attire, fierce aspect, drawn swords, and screaming, prancing horses rendered them somewhat incongruous companions for a young lady's morning canter. It seemed, therefore, in no way strange for their party to assume the aspect of a military expedition. Boldero, however, added all the civil splendour at his command, and called into requisition all the resources of the District officer's establishment to make Maud's journey luxurious.

All along their route there were signs of due preparation for the 'Deputy Commissioner Sahib's' party. Whenever they came to a halting-place they found a little encampment of tents already pitched, surrounded by a host of willing ministrants; a meal awaiting them, the teakettle simmering or champagne cooling, and all the little comforts that Indian servants have so ready a knack of extemporising on a march. Maud, though still weak, had sufficiently recovered to enjoy it all extremely, and found her companion very much to her taste, yet not altogether as she would have him.   He watched over her with as anxious and tender a care as Sutton himself could have done.   Everything that could by any possibility contribute to her comfort had evidently been thought of with a sedulous attention.   Thus dinner each evening was a little banquet of a very different description from the rough-and-ready meal which sufficed for Boldero's simple tastes on ordinary occasions.   Maud's every wish was watched.   Twenty miles from home she had said casually that she had left her scent-bottle behind her, and thought no more of it till it made its appearance next morning at breakfast.   Horsemen had been riding through the night in order that she might not lack her eau de Cologne. Sutton had insisted on sending with her his own especial body-servant, who had been with him ever since he was a lad, and was, Maud knew, essential to the comfort of his existence. He might, however, have spared himself the sacrifice, for Boldero provèd himself a brilliant organiser, and was full of resources. Maud simply rode from one pleasant drawing-room to another. The journey kept her in a glow of pleasure. 'How pretty it is!' she cried, as they alighted after the first morning's march, and found the camp-fires alight, the relays of ponies picketed, and a banquet ready under a vast peepul-tree's shade. 'How pretty it is, and how good you are to me! I am beginning to feel like an Eastern queen on a royal progress.'

'Pray rule us as you will,' said Boldero, gallantly. 'You will find us loyal subjects. Meanwhile, let your Majesty's cup-bearer offer you some hock and Seltzer-water, the best of beverages after a thirsty ride.'

But, polite and kind and patient as Boldero was, he was yet not quite as Maud would have him.   His mirth, formerly so ready and unconstrained, had departed.   He made no approach to familiarity, scarcely to unconstraint.   He was ready to talk, if she began the conversation ; but he was equally well pleased to ride for miles without a word. His object seemed to be to make her journey pleasant, but he gave no symptom that it pleased himself.   He never for a moment forgot that she was the Colonel's lady, and he the District officer in attendance upon her.   It jarred somehow with Maud's idea of what was interesting, natural, romantic. Many nice men, most nice men, she thought, were eager in rushing into friendship with her, and required a little putting down. It was provoking that Boldero showed no tendency to stand in need of this gentle repression. She had liked him especially last year, and he had seemed quite alive and responsive to the fact; now it piqued her that, beyond the assiduous politeness required by his position as a host, he showed no symptom of being fascinated; in plain language he quite declined to flirt, and yet she gave him every opportunity. This was provoking, since Maud herself felt especially disposed to be gracious.

'Now,' she said, after luncheon, when Boldero showed symptoms of retreating, 'please do not go away to smoke; let us sit in this pleasant shade—you shall read me some poetry—no, if you please, you may smoke, and I will read to you. See, now, I

have my beloved Browning—I am so fond of
this.' And Maud began to read, which she
did very nicely :—

> Constance, I know not how it is with men :
> For women (I am a woman now like you)
> There is no good of life but love—but love !
> What else looks good, is some shade flung from love ;
> Love gilds it, gives it worth. Be warned by me,
> Never you cheat yourself one instant ! Love,
> Give love, and only love, and leave the rest !

'Will you have some more of this hock
before it is packed up ?' said Boldero, in the
most determined manner.

'No, thank you,' said Maud, with a sigh
of real annoyance, 'I will not have any
more hock before it is packed up, nor shall
you have any more poetry. And why, kind
Fates, is it that I have so prosaic a companion for my journey, just when I happen
to feel poetical ?'

'It was because the prosy companion

happened to be going at the right moment,' Boldero said. 'I am afraid this sounds very unromantic too, but I advise you to go into the tent and have a thorough rest before we start again. And, by the way, I shall be sending back to the camp : do you want to write a line to Sutton ? '

'Of all things !' cried Maud. 'And I shall tell him how pleasant you have been about the poetry.'

Before their Elysian residence was reached Maud discovered that it was Boldero's particular function to recal her husband to her thoughts : sometimes at moments when oblivion would have been preferable.

CHAPTER XXXII.

A GRASS WIDOW.

Now simmer blinks on flowery braes,
And o'er the crystal streamlet plays,
Come let us spend the lightsome days
  In the Birks of Aberfeldy.

The braes ascend like lofty wa's,
The foaming stream deep roaring fa's,
 O'erhung wi' fragrant spreading shaws,
  The Birks of Aberfeldy.
Bonnie lassie, will ye go, will ye go, will ye go,
Bonnie lassie, will ye go to the Birks of Aberfeldy?

MAUD found Mrs. Vereker's promises of hospitality and enjoyment fully verified. The
change from the Camp was delightful; the
extra four thousand feet of altitude made life
a luxury. Energy, in a hundred different
forms, returned to her: some new spring of

life quickened her powers alike of mind and body. Mere existence once again became delightful ; the pleasant consciousness of health and strength again put her in high spirits. The dull routine in which she had been living of late seemed very dull. She missed her husband, and wrote him enthusiastic letters to tell him so ; but a hundred fresh pleasures and interests rushed in to fill the vacant space and to deaden the feeling of regret. And then it had been settled that as soon as the inspection was finished Sutton should get leave to come up and write his report at Elysium, so that their separation promised to be a very short one.

Mrs. Vereker's cottage was the scene of a great many quiet but enjoyable festivities. She had the most charming little luncheon parties, over which she presided with a modesty, liveliness, and grace which her guests found irresistible. There was not much to eat, but each one in his turn received a smile and a glance from the purple eyes, and found his glass of sherry turning into nectar before him. These happy guests were mostly military; and he must have been a severe critic indeed who would have denied them the merit of fault-less attire, good looks, and chivalrous dispo-sitions. The very atmosphere was infectious with flirtation. Mrs. Vereker kept a little court of gentlemen, each with his ac-knowledged position in the hierarchy of adorers; nor did she appear to question that her guest would do the same. She took for granted that Maud would accept Desvœux's proffered politeness; she laughed a little gentle laugh at her girlish scruples, and turned her sweet eyes upon her in amused wonderment at such innocent prudery.

'My dear child,' she said, 'what are we poor wives to do? Sit, with our hands crossed, singing hymns, and thinking of our *cari sposi* in the Plains? How would my good man be the better if I went out moping for rides all alone, instead of being attended by my cavalier? Besides, no one ever would believe that one was alone, and one would be gossiped about as much as ever. And then did not your old Othello wish that Boldero was here to look after you? No, no, I don't find " moping " among the other disagreeable things we vowed to do when matrimony marked us for its own. And then you must know that three is quite an impossible number at the Hills—the paths are too narrow, happily—and three is an odious number, which ought to be turned out of the arithmetic-books. So you must start a flirtation not to interfere with mine. Besides, Mr. Desvœux is too charming. I only wish that he would flirt with me!'

So Maud found herself taken possession of by Desvœux, and assigned to him as a matter of course in the set in which she was living. The worst of it was that she found it rather pleasant. It was, of course, convenient to have some one ready to fetch and carry, who was always on the look-out for one at parties, and only too delighted at having any command to obey. It was all above-board, and recognised as right. Everyone knew that there was not the least harm in it. The only drawback was that Maud found it very difficult to describe the state of things to Jem, and her letters grew shorter than was right. Mrs. Vereker was too volatile, too frivolous, too much in love with herself and the world around her, , to allow of her companion lapsing into a serious mood. She spent hours over a succession of toilettes, each of which was perfection; hours more in designing how such perfection should be achieved. High spirits and fun pervaded her every thought, but dress was the matter about which Mrs. Vereker was most nearly feeling serious. The two ladies had a long discussion over the attire which would do most justice to their charms at the Viceroy's Fancy Ball.

'I can't go as a Marquise,' said Mrs. Vereker, 'because powder does not set my eyes off well, and paint spoils my complexion. I mean to be Night—holy, peaceful Night—black tulle, you know, with a crescent moon glittering on my forehead, and little diamond stars twinkling, twinkling in both my ears, which you know are loves.   See, now !'   And Mrs. Vereker caught up a great piece of muslin which was lying on the sofa, threw it over her shoulders, turned her beautiful violet eyes to the ceiling, and went sliding across the room with a sweet, demure smile and graceful undulations.

'See, now !' she cried.   'Don't you feel the moonlight and the nightingales and the tinkling folds, and how very sacred and peaceful it all is ?   I shall be furious if at least sixteen men don't break their hearts about me.   But, my dear, you shall be a *vivandière*, and show your pretty ankles ; or a Normandy flower-girl, with a high cap and crimson petticoat.   Or why not be Morning, and dance in my quadrille; a Rising Sun, with rays?'

'Oh, no, thank you,' Maud answered; 'I intend to have a quadrille of my own. I leave you the sun, moon, and stars to yourself. Mr. Desvœux is arranging one for me out of Sir Walter Scott; something historical and romantic.'

Then Desvœux would come (oftener than ever, since this Historical Quadrille gave a new excuse for frequent calls) and turn everything into ridicule. 'As usual,' he told them, 'Mrs. Fotheringham has been trying to drive a bargain. The two young ladies are to go as Mediæval Princesses; and poor Giroflont, who had come all the way from Calcutta to dress the ladies' hair for the Fancy Ball, stipulated for his accustomed

five rupees a-head. Fotheringham *mère* stuck
out for three. Giroflont rejected the suggestion with scorn. "Impossible, madame,"
he said, "ce sont des coiffures historiques!"
So exit Mrs. Fotheringham in a fury.'

'And the poor girls will have to go as
milkmaids,' said Mrs. Vereker. 'What a
shame! And what a mother!'

'And what a father!' said Desvœux.
'He has just been to interview the Agent,
and has made us both extremely ill. Such
vapid dulness!

> He spoke of virtue—not the gods
> More purely when they wish to charm
> Pallas and Juno sitting by;
> And with a sweeping of the arm,
> And a lack-lustre dead-blue eye
> Devolved his rounded periods.

'What a comfort you must find it, Mr.
Desvœux,' said Mrs. Vereker, 'to fly for
refuge to eyes that are neither lack-lustre

nor dead-blue! Now I come to think of it, though, I believe dead-blue is just the shade of mine.'

'Yours!' said Desvœux, in a tone of fervour which spoke volumes.

'Those poor girls!' cried Maud, 'how shamefully they are dressed! Perfect quakeresses!'

'Quakeresses!' answered Desvœux. 'But quakeresses are too charming; dear little tender doves, in the softest silk and freshest muslin. I suffered agonies once upon a time on account of one.'

'Profane!' cried Mrs. Vereker. 'Quakers are really a sort of monks and nuns, only that they happen to have husbands and wives.'

'Yes,' said Desvœux, 'monasticism without its single recommendation!'

'Rude man!' Mrs. Vercker cried. 'Let us send him away, Maud. I should like to know, sir, what would become of you without us married women?'

'What indeed?' cried Desvœux. 'But, you know, when the Pope offered Petrarch a dispensation to marry he declined, on the ground that he could not write poetry to his wife.'

'That reminds me,' said Mrs. Vereker, 'that I must write some prose to my husband, and Mrs. Sutton some to hers; and the post goes in half-an-hour. Mr. Desvœux, you must really go.'

'I obey,' said Desvœux, with a sigh. 'My exile from paradise is cheered by the thought that I am coming back at four to take Mrs. Sutton for a ride.'

CHAPTER XXXIII.

FACILIS DESCENSUS AVERNI.

Birds, yet in freedom, shun the net
Which Love around your haunts hath set.

THE pleasant weeks flew by, a round of enjoyments. Maud found herself in great request. She and Mrs. Vereker held quite a little levée every morning. Day after day a never-failing stream of visitors poured along the path to the modest but picturesque residence where these two beauties waited to charm mankind. The grass-plot in front was worn quite bare by a succession of ponies, who waited there while their owners were worshipping within.

No young officer who arrived for a holiday considered himself at all *en règle* till he
had been to pay his respects to this adorable
couple.

Mrs. Vereker was none the less at-
tractive, as she knew very well, for being
contrasted with another charming woman,
whose charms were of a different order.
'Blest pair of syrens!' Desvœux used to
say in his impudent fashion; 'it is too
charming to have you both together—a
dangerous conspiracy against the peace of
mind of one-half of the species.'

'Ah!' Mrs. Vereker would answer, turning her violet eyes upon him, with a sweet
reproachful smile, which would have melted
any heart but Desvœux's; 'and when one
of the syrens is young and lovely, and just
arrived from the Plains.   There *were* days,

my dear Maud, when Mr. Desvœux used
to want to ride with me, and used to run my
errands so nicely! Alas! alas! for mascu-
line weathercocks! I am very jealous of
you, my dear, I'd have you to know, and
shall, some day, tear your pretty eyes out.
You do too much execution by half. Meanwhile, here is my dear General Beau coming
up the road.'

Maud shrugged her shoulders and arched
her pretty brow, and both Desvœux and
Mrs. Vereker burst out laughing to see the
General portrayed.

'The General to the life!' cried Desvœux, '"like a poet or peer,

> With his arched eyebrow and Parnassian sneer."'

'I protest against the poet,' cried Mrs.
Vereker, laughing. 'We always flirt in the

very plainest prose. As for his eyebrows,
they are adorable.'

Then the General arrived, as great a
dandy as ever Poole turned out, and was in
the drawing-room before Maud's gravity was
at all re-established. 'And what was the
laugh about?' he enquired.

'About a Parnassian sneer,' said Desvœux, with great presence of mind. 'And
where do you come from, General?'

'I have been calling at the Fotheringhams',' said the General. 'My intimacy with
Mrs. Fotheringham does not incline me to
wish to be one of her daughters.'

'Poor girls!' said Mrs. Vereker, 'we
were commiserating them the other day,
and saying how cruelly their mother treats
them.'

'Ah!' said the General, 'she does indeed;

actually makes the poor things do lessons all the morning. A certain gentleman, a friend of mine, I cannot tell you his name, went there the other day with the most serious intentions towards the little one, the one with yellow hair, and actually found them hard at work at Mill's " Logic." '

' Two women were grinding at the mill,' said Desvœux, 'and one was taken and the other left, I suppose ? '

' I am afraid,' said Mrs. Vereker, ' that both were left. But fancy a woman who was also a logician ! For my part I consider it a great privilege to be as unreasonable as I choose.'

' The arguments of beauty,' said the General, 'are always irresistible ; but I am quite for female education.'

' And I,' said Mrs. Vereker, ' am dead

against it. We know quite as much as is
good for us as it is. What do you say,
Maud ? '

' I have quite forgotten all I learnt at
school already,' said Maud. ' General Beau,
can you say your Duty to your Neighbour ? '

' And your duty to your neighbour's
wife ? ' put in Desvœux. ' But I object to
all education as revolutionary—part of this
horrid radical epoch in which we live.'

' Yes,' said Mrs. Vereker, ' one of the
nice things about India is its being a military despotism. As for Europe, the mobs
have it all their own way.'

' Horrid mobs !' said Desvœux, ' as if an
unwashed rabble was Nature's last achievement.

Her 'prentice hand she tried on lords,
And then she made the masses O !'

'But you must teach them religion, you know,' said the General, 'the Catechism, and so forth.'

'Of course,' said Maud; 'their Duty to their Neighbour, for instance.'

'I don't know,' said Mrs. Vereker; 'they only have it all by rote. When I was last in England our clergyman gave us this specimen of one of his parishioners, to whom he had been detailing the mysteries of faith :

' "*Clergyman.* And now, Sally, how do you expect to be saved ?"

' "*Sally.* Dun'noa ; please, sir, tell I."

'Well,' said Desvœux, 'theology is a thing I never could understand myself. Now I must be off to my Agent.'

'When shall we see you again ?' said Maud.

' Dun'noa,' said Desvœux ; 'please, ma'am,

tell I. What time shall I come and take you out this afternoon ?'

But the ladies had visitors more distinguished even than the General. The Agent himself came in one Sunday after church, and asked to be allowed to stay to lunch. Cards flowed in apace from Government House, for the Master of the Ceremonies there knew that no entertainment would be complete where Maud was not.

There were little dances got up expressly in her honour, for which her card of engagements was filled for days before : at every point homage the sweetest that woman's ears can listen to awaited her. A chorus of worshippers assured her she was beautiful ; the incense was for ever burning on her shrine, till the very air became drugged with flattery. Yet Maud was not completely happy; her conscience was ill at ease. The scene around her was pleasant; but, tried by certain standards, she knew that it would fall short. She remembered, with a sigh, the sort of way in which her cousin Vernon would have turned up his nose at the people among whom she was living, and she knew that in many ways they deserved it. Felicia, she knew, thought Mrs. Vereker utterly frivolous, fast, and slightly vulgar, and she felt that Felicia was right. Her husband, conscience reminded her, disapproved of and despised Desvœux; and was there not something to disapprove and dislike about him? Still Maud felt the consequence was that she had fallen out of harmony with those stricter judges whose tastes just now it was convenient to forget. It gave her no pleasure to think of them. She fancied Jem in a silently reproachful mood, Felicia daintily contemptuous, Vernon with an outspoken sneer. Her letters to her husband, though they never contained the hundred-thousandth part of one untruth, began to be less faithful and complete transcripts of her life than of old. Desvœux ought, in truth, to have occupied a more prominent place. She felt ashamed to tell her husband, toiling hard in solitude and heat, of the round of gaiety in which her life was passed. On the other hand, her husband's letters gave her no satisfaction. They were far from amusing; indeed, the life which he was leading was hardly susceptible, in livelier hands than his, of being rendered amusing or picturesque. He missed her, of course; but then he would be with her again in a few weeks, and Maud did not think it necessary to be sentimental about it. His pen was far from a ready one, and this Report, Maud knew, would be worse to him than a campaign. In his letters to her his one idea would have been to conceal from her anything that was disagreeable, and she might, if she had chosen, have augured ill from his reticence; but life just now was too bright and exciting for such inward monition to get a hearing. Her companions had infected her with a passion for pleasure, and duty had faded into indistinctness. Then, too, her new position as a married lady and as Sutton's bride was not without its charm. She was a much grander lady now than she had been the year before as Miss Vernon, and this access of dignity was pleasurable. It involved, however, being taken in to dinner by officials of an age, dignity, and disposition which she found anything but congenial to her own, though Desvœux protested that she was trying to establish a flirtation with the Agent. Once at Government House she had the honour of sitting next the Viceroy, an alarming but yet delightful eminence. How kind he seemed, how full of friendly talk, how eager to know about her husband and his doings!

'How is your *preux chevalier*?' he said. 'What would become of everything, I wonder, in that stormy corner that he keeps in such good order, but for him? He is one of the people whom I completely trust.'

Maud felt her cheek glowing with a pleasure, yet the pleasure was not without a sting. Everybody conspired to speak of her husband as some one beyond the usual flight in goodness, chivalry, nobility of soul. Was she behaving as became the wife of such a man? Was she loving, honouring, and obey- ing in the full spirit of her vow? Was it honourable or right, that half-a-dozen foolish lads should be competing for familiarity with her, and a man like Desvœux be her usual companion? Ought her husband to hear such things of her? This was the little skeleton which Maud kept locked up, along with many lovely dresses, in her bedroom closet, this the little prick her conscience gave her, this the drop of bitter in the glittering ambrosial draught of pleasure.

She drank it all the same, and found it too sweet to put it from her lips.

CHAPTER XXXIV.

BAD TIMES IN THE PLAINS.

Where nature sickens, and each air is death.

WHILE the fortunate Elysians were thus
bravely keeping up their own and one
another's spirits by a round of gaieties, the
people in the Plains were busy with a round
of work of quite a different description.
Cholera having broken out, all leave in the
infected regiments had been cancelled, and
many a luckless officer had come back to
his cantonment, grumbling at a curtailed
holiday and the stern mandate which recalled him just as he had reached the snow

scenery of which he had dreamed for months, or established himself in some happy hunting-ground for a two months' campaign against ibex or bison. Back they all came, however, poor fellows, to take their equal chance with rank-and-file against an enemy of whom even the bravest men are not ashamed to be afraid

The prevalence of illness, and the pre-cautions ordered to prevent its increase, entailed a deal of extra labour, and kept all the officers busily employed. The hospitals required constant visiting, for the men were moody and disheartened, and stood in need of all the encouragement that their leaders could give them. Sutton, always thinking of everyone but himself, had ordered two of his 'boys' away to an outpost forty miles off, nominally to look after a turbulent Zámindar, really to be out of harm's way. This threw all the more work on his hands, and it was work that he felt himself specially capable of doing with good effect. His visits at the hospital were, he knew, eagerly looked for, and a few kind words from the Colonel Sahib often inspired cheerfulness and hope at a moment when gloom and despondency were telling with mortal effect on men's minds and bodies. His regiment had already lost several men, and they had died happy in the thought that the well-loved leader was ever close at hand, and ever on the look-out for something to alleviate their suffering. Many a gaunt visage, with death already written in each ghastly feature, lighted up with sudden brightness as he came, and, when exhaustion had gone too far for speech, smiled him a heartfelt benediction of gratitude and love. The scene was, indeed, one full of pathos, even to a less interested looker-on than the Colonel. It was horrible to see these sturdy, joyous, much-enduring, dare-devil troopers lying so utterly prostrated, unnerved, and helpless. Death, it seemed, should have come to them in the form of steel or bullet, the thrust of lance, the crashing sword-cut or wild cavalry charge; not as a pestilence, creeping on them unawares, and slaying them in their beds. Sutton, who had looked death in the face a hundred times with perfect indifference, began to understand why people feared it. After all, some aspects of life are, he felt, too delightful to leave without a sigh. For the last few months he had been, for the first time in his life, completely happy. A new era had begun for him, new vistas of pleasure had opened up. All that had gone before had been duty, excitement, hard work ; not, indeed, without its enjoyment, but, after all, something far from happiness in the sense in which Sutton had now begun to understand it. Fighting was all well enough, and the hazardous ambition of a soldier's career delightfully spirit-stirring, but it was not here that the real end of life was to be found. Sutton's real end of life was now the little being who was flirting away at the Hills, in happy forgetfulness of all but the present moment. Sutton, however, thought of her only as he had seen her, tender, affectionate, devoted to himself. Since the half-quarrel about her departure- for the Hills, and the reconciliation which followed it, his life with her had been one of perfect happiness. Maud had been raised by her

conquest over herself into a sweeter, nobler
mood, and was more than ever mistress of
her husband's heart. Her departure, pe-
remptorily insisted on by her husband, had
none the less cost them both a bitter pang ;
though Sutton promised that it should be for
a few weeks at the utmost, a promise which
cheered Maud more than it did himself, as
she knew not, as he did, how easily its
fulfilment might be rendered impossible. So
Sutton went about his work in his own
determined, loyal fashion, but with his heart
no longer in it. His treasure was elsewhere,
and his heart with it. The collection of
materials for his Report gave him a deal of
trouble, and involved many weary rides.
He had to see District officers, Zámindars,
police inspectors, heads of villages, spies,
and then to determine what the real neces-

sities of the case were, and where the posts should be fixed. Everything depended on his work being well, wisely, and thoroughly done. The responsibility weighed on him : the peace, safety, prosperity of a whole District was hanging on his judgment. This is the kind of work which tries conscientious and loyal men far more than physical exertion. Then the cholera, which had shown symptoms of abatement, broke out all of a sudden with more violence than ever, and it became apparent that Sutton's regiment was thoroughly infected. Then all real hopes of his getting up to the Hills for the present, at any rate, had to be abandoned ; but of this he said nothing to his wife. It was of no use to distress her beforehand with bad news, which she would be certain to learn quite soon enough.

One evening, when Sutton had returned, thoroughly tired with a long, hot expedition, the orderly, whose task it was to bring him the returns of the sick for the day, told him that in the list of seizures for that afternoon was a Pathan boy, who had been picked up years before by some of the troopers in a suddenly deserted village, and who had lived as a pet child of the regiment ever since. Sutton had been kind to the lad, had defrayed such small charges as his maintenance in the lines involved, and had secured him the beginning of an education in the regimental school. Sutton went off at once to the hospital. Already the disease had made fearful progress, and he saw in a moment that the boy was in the most critical condition. He bent over the exhausted, helpless form, and said a few kind words of hopefulness and sympathy. The boy listened with glistening eyes and lips quivering with agitation; and as Sutton turned to go he sprang up in bed, forgetful of everything but the master-feeling which overpowered him, and clasped his protector round the neck with a single outburst of affection : ' Ma-Bap,' ' My father and mother !'

Two hours later they came to say that the boy was dead, and before the next morning Sutton began to be aware that that last embrace had been a deadly one, and that the dread malady had laid its hand upon himself.

CHAPTER XXXV.

AN ELYSIAN PICNIC.

Nay, the world—the world,
All ear and eye, with such a stupid heart
To interpret ear and eye, and such a tongue
To blaze its own interpretation !

THREE gallant officers, who had been en-
joying the hospitality of Elysium for many
weeks, were fired one day with the noble
resolve to show their gratitude to the gentlemen, and their devotion to the ladies, by
whom they had been so pleasantly enter-
tained. It was an inspiration, everybody felt
at once, and all Elysium thrilled with conscious responsiveness at the happy thought.
There is a little valley near Elysium, a mile

or two from the mountain's summit, where a green, smooth sward invites the weary climber to repose ; where venerable deodars, towering on the steep hillside, stretch their limbs to ward off the fierce afternoon sun ; where a headlong stream comes bubbling down among the thick-grown ferns and falls in a feathery cascade and disappears in the gorge below ; where the Genius of the Mountains has, in fact, its chosen haunt. There you may sit and watch the rose-tipped snowy range warming into fresh life and beauty as the sun goes down, and fading into cold gloom as he disappears. Here, in a hundred suggestive nooks, Nature has hinted at a sylvan tête-à-tête, or spread a verdant curtain of wild growth to festoon an al fresco banquet ; and here it was that the three inspired officers resolved to give an

entertainment that should at once do justice
to the warmth of their feelings, the correct-
ness of their tastes, and the profuseness of
their liberality.

It was to be a picnic—the picnic of the
season—the picnic of the world ; and if en-
chanting scenery, a cloudless sky, enthusiastic
hosts, a crowd of pretty women, an army of
devoted men, a community not too blasé to
be easily amused, nor yet so unused to
pleasure as not to know how to take it—if all
these ingredients, backed with the music of a
lovely band crashing out among the rocks ;
cookery over which, by gracious permission,
the Viceroy's own chef presided ; and champagne iced to perfection in Himalayan snows,
could make a success, then it would, as
Maud expected, be indeed an era in the
lives of all concerned.

Mrs. Vereker (though perhaps less sanguine than her more youthful companion) determined to have a new dress for the occasion, and a committee of adorers discussed the rival merits of half-a-dozen projected costumes. Mrs. Vereker, however, treated all their suggestions with contempt, and determined in the depths of her own consciousness on something that should be a sweet surprise.

Maud, happily, had one of her English treasures which was still unknown to the admiring public, and which she felt at once would be the very thing.

For some days nothing but the picnic could be talked of in Elysium ; what to wear at it, how to get to it, how to return, were topics of the liveliest interest to all. A hundred pleasant plans in connection with it shaped themselves into being. General Beau, who liked being beforehand with the world, secured for himself the honour of escorting Mrs. Vereker ; and Desvœux, as a matter of course, established his claim to act as Maud's gentleman-in-waiting on the occasion. By this time her spirits were very high and impatient of all that seemed to check their flow. She was flirting with Desvœux, she knew, in the most open manner, yet she resented any notice being taken of it. Boldero had met her at a croquet-party and been very disagreeable. He confessed to having been two days in Elysium, and could or would give no account of why he had not been to call. ' How unkind and unlike the old Mr. Boldero whom we all liked so much ! How you are changed ! '

' Yes,' Boldero said, flushing up quite red,

so that Maud knew that he meant more than met the ear, 'and some one else is changed too, and might not care about her former friends.'

'What do you mean?' Maud said, disturbed at Boldero's serious air. 'How can I care about you, if you won't come and see me? Come, now, and take me across the lawn for an ice, and tell me what it is that is the matter.'

'I do not think I can tell you,' said Boldero, greatly alarmed at finding himself committed to a lecture. 'You will not like it; you want a scolding.'

'Well,' said Maud, 'I like scoldings from my friends, and I often deserve them; and often get them, goodness knows. Give me one now; only you must be quick, please, because there is Mr. Desvœux signalling me, and I have promised to go for a ride with him.'

' Don't,' said Boldero, with great alacrity. ' Stay and hear my lecture. Let me go and say you would rather not.'

' Not for the world !' cried Maud. ' I am looking forward to it immensely ; he would be broken-hearted if I disappointed him, poor fellow. How would you like it yourself ? '

' Broken-hearted !' said Boldero, with that peculiar turn of contempt in his voice with which her husband and his friends always vexed Maud by speaking of Des-vœux.

' How disagreeable you are !' said Maud. ' Don't you know he is my particular friend ? '

' Friend !' said Boldero. ' He is the very worst enemy you have, believe me. For-give me, as your husband's old friend, if I

tell you the truth when, it seems, no one else
will. He is making you talked of ; and if
you could only know how people talk ! He
knows it, and he likes it, and it is what he
is always doing.'

'And what you are always doing,' said
Maud, in a passion, 'is coming and saying
the most horrid things in the most disagreeable way, and joining the horrid people who
gossip about one. Do they talk of me ?
Then why dont you make them eat their
words—you, who used to be my friend ?'

'I am your friend,' said the other, with a
grave persistence, 'and Sutton's too. It is
because I am, that I risk your displeasure
by telling you that you are doing wrong.'

'Doing wrong ?' cried Maud, by this
time quite flushed with excitement, and
hardly mistress of her words. 'How dare

you say so? You know it is false. I am alone, or you would not dare to insult me.'

'Come,' said Boldero, unmoved by the taunt, of which Maud herself felt the outrageous injustice, 'be sensible, and let me take care of you this evening—do me a kind act for once.'

'Thank you,' said Maud, the tears gleaming in her eyes; 'and hear such things as you have been saying over again? Take care of me, indeed! Please never speak to me again!'

She was gone, leaving her companion discomfited. In another instant Desvœux was at her side, and, as he lifted her to her pony, said something which made her laugh and blush. Boldero would have liked to throttle him.

Maud's conscience, however, prevented her full enjoyment of the ride. She knew as well as possible that Boldero was telling her truth : she *was* doing wrong, she felt only too distinctly. Boldero would have cut his fingers off to please her, and she had chosen to misunderstand him. Still it was too provoking to be lectured. When she got home there was a letter from Dustypore, which told her that Felicia too had heard of her proceedings, and was wanting to warn her. ' You must not forget, dear Maud,' the letter said, ' what a home of gossip Elysium is, and how all that is young and pretty and interesting, is what gossip busies itself most about. Some men, like Mr. Desvœux, for instance, have only to look at one for the gossipers to begin ; but I know you will be very judicious, even at the expense of being somewhat too particular. How I wish I were with you!'

'They all want to tease me with their horrid advice and hints,' Maud thought, in vexation of heart. 'As for Mr. Boldero, he was too odious : I can never, never forgive him.'

Then, as if all the world were in a conspiracy, Mrs. Fotheringham, whom Maud met at a dinner-party that night, pounced upon her as the ladies were filing into the drawing-room and made her come and sit down on a remote sofa.

Maud always believed, probably not without justice, that Mrs. Fotheringham bore her a grudge for being married before the two Misses Fotheringham : she was, accordingly, quite indisposed to be lectured.

' My dear,' Mrs. Fotheringham said, ' an

old woman may sometimes give a young one a friendly hint. You don't know the world as I do, with my twenty years of India. Now, don't be angry with me if I give you a bit of advice. Take care! Young wives whose husbands are in the Plains cannot take too much.'

This seemed the last drop in the over-flowing cup of annoyance and humiliation. Maud felt excessively indignant. It was an impertinence surely for Mrs. Fotheringham to venture to speak so.

'And what am I to take care of?' she said. 'And what right have you to speak to me in this way?'

'Take care of your companions, my dear. You have chosen the most dangerous, the worst you could find—Mr. Desvœux.'

'Stop, stop!' cried Maud, jumping up in

a fury. ' He is my friend ; my kind friend. I will not hear him abused.'

' You must be on your guard,' continued the other, with exasperating pertinacity. ' He is very unprincipled.'

' I know he is very agreeable,' cried Maud. ' Unprincipled ! What do you mean by that ? '

' I mean—I mean,' said the other, ' that he is dangerous—just the sort of man to try to kiss you, if you gave him the chance.'

' Indeed ? ' cried Maud, by this time in far too great a passion to be either courteous or discreet. ' I should think none the worse of him for that. *I believe they all would !* '

Having delivered this parting shot, Maud hurried away, in a great state of agitation, and Mrs. Fotheringham shrugged her shoulders in despair at so unseemly an outburst of temper; so awful a view of human nature.

When they got home that night Maud told Mrs. Vereker her troubles, and was relieved to find what slight importance she attached to them.   She burst out laughing, and clapped her hands in delight at Maud's account of the encounter with Mrs. Fotheringham. 'But, my dear child, what induced you to make such a foolish speech?   And as for Mr. Boldero, he wanted you himself, don't you understand?   Flirt a little with *him* to-morrow, and see how much he will want to lecture you then.'

'But he won't flirt with me,' said Maud. 'It is very odd.   Besides, I was in a passion, and told him never to speak to me again. Poor fellow!'

'You dear little goose!' Mrs. Vereker

said, kissing her, 'sit down this instant. Write and tell him you are broken-hearted for being so rude, and that he is to come to lunch and finish his lecture to-morrow. You must not quarrel with all the world at once.'

Of Felicia's letter Mrs. Vereker equally made light. 'She means nothing, my dear, except what I preach to you and practise myself, discretion and moderation. So many dances in the evening, so many rides in the week, so many lunches, so many looks, so many smiles, and so forth. Besides, you know, Mrs. Vernon is a prude, a born prude, she breathes a' congenial atmosphere of proprieties where I should be suffocated. She likes men to be polite, and only polite; I take them up where politeness ends and something else begins. She likes small-beer; I happen to prefer champagne, bright, sparkling, and intoxicatingly delicious! Besides,' rattled on Mrs. Vereker, quite at ease with a familiar topic, ' Mrs. Vernon is a flirt too, in her prudish way. She flirts, she used to flirt with your husband scandalously. I hope he behaves better now. Mine is a monster, and makes me cry my eyes out. But, I tell you what, my dear Maud : there is great safety in numbers. Don't speak to that saucy Desvœux for a fortnight, and turn your pretty eyes on some one else, the first you fancy. Would you like my General ? or Parson Boldero ? Take him in hand, my dear, and in a week we will make the horrid fellow flirt just as much as his neighbours.'

' He's a very bad hand at it at present,' said Maud, with a laugh.

However, the result of the conference was

that Maud sat down and wrote a pretty little
repentant note ; and the next day Boldero
came with a beating heart and took the little
scapegrace for a ride, and scolded her very
affectionately, much to his own satisfaction,
through a whole pleasant summer afternoon.

CHAPTER XXXVI.

A KISS.

As she sped fast through sun and shade
The happy winds upon her played,
Blowing the ringlet from the braid;
She looked so lovely as she swayed
      The rein with dainty finger-tips.

A man had given all other bliss
And all his worldly worth for this :
To waste his whole heart in one kiss
      Upon her perfect lips.

WHEN Mrs. Vereker suggested Desvœux's temporary deposition she overlooked two obstacles which proved fatal to the scheme's success : in the first place, Maud did not quite wish to depose him; in the next, Desvœux had not the slightest intention of being deposed. Despite all hints to stay away, he presented himself with provoking regularity at Mrs. Vereker's cottage-porch, outstayed later callers without the least compunction, and evidently felt himself quite master of the situation.

At Maud's first symptom of neglect he was more devoted, more assiduous, more amusing than ever. Both ladies were constrained in their hearts to admit that his presence was a great enlivenment. Maud, though she would not have admitted it to herself, felt sometimes impatient for his arrival. She had given Desvœux to understand that his attentions were unwelcome, but she had not the least wish that he should become inattentive. As the French song says :—

Lorsque l'on dit, ' Ne m'aimez plus jamais,'
On prétend bien qu'on obéira, mais
On compte un peu sur des révoltes.

So Maud, when she tried to keep Desvœux at a distance, probably only made it apparent how much she liked him to be near ; at any rate, the attempt at a little quarrel had only the result of making them better friends than before.   Then there was a sort of familiarity about him which Maud was conscious of only half-disliking.   Mrs. Vereker declared she had not breathed a word ; but something in his look, when he spoke of Mrs. Fothering-ham, convinced Maud that he had heard of her unlucky speech to that lady.   When she rode with some one else she was sure to meet him, looking the picture of dulness. She knew that if they had been together they would be both having the greatest fun.   And then how flat and what a bore her own companion seemed !   One day she did

actually go for a ride with General Beau.
Mrs. Vereker asked him afterwards how
they had got on, and the General arched
his brow and said, 'Ah!' in a manner which
suggested that he had not altogether liked
it. Then, one day, in a pet, Maud went out
alone, saying, 'No one can find fault with me
for *this.*' Alas! alas! she was sauntering
along in the most disconsolate manner, when,
round a corner of the hill, who should come
sauntering along but Desvœux, also alone
and disconsolate, and in the direst need of
a companion! Of course under such circumstances there was nothing to be done but
for Desvœux to turn his pony round and
accompany her for the rest of the expedition ; and then, no sooner had they done
this, than, as bad luck would have it, they

came upon all the people whom they particularly did not wish to meet—first the Fotheringhams, the mamma and two young ladies in jampans, a nice young civilian escorting each; Fotheringham *père*, on his pony, bringing up the rear—in order, as Desvœux said scornfully, to cut off retreat if the young men's hearts failed them.

'If that is courtship *à la mode*,' he said, 'heaven preserve us! Fancy four parental eyes glaring at every act! My love is a sensitive plant, and would shrink up at every look.'

Maud, however, felt that it was no joke, and was very much provoked with Desvœux. She was in the act of turning back to join the Fotheringhams.

'Don't, pray don't,' said Desvœux; '*qui s'excuse s'accuse*. Why don't the two young gentlemen come and ask to be allowed to walk with us and be taken care of ? If only we could *afficher*

'"MET BY ACCIDENT,

UPON OUR HONOUR,"

on our backs, and let all the world know how innocent we really are!'

And next, before Maud had at all recovered her equanimity, a turn in the road brought them face to face with all the Government House party, ladies, and ponies, and aides-de-camp in attendance, and, last of all, the Viceroy himself, with a big stick and wide-awake hat. 'Ah! how d'ye do, Mrs. Sutton?' he said, looking, Maud fancied, not near so good-humoured as of old, and taking no notice of Desvœux. 'I hope you have good accounts of your husband?'

'Yes, very good, thank you, Lord Clare,' Maud said, blushing at a question which seemed to convey a reproach to her guilty conscience, and at the thought of how little her husband had been present to her mind of late. Altogether, Maud's attempt at a solitary ride turned out a thorough failure.

Then came the picnic, and Maud, it must be confessed, behaved like a little idiot.

'The best way to treat gossip,' Desvœux suggested, 'is to ignore it, and show the world that you have nothing to be ashamed of.' By way of enforcing his doctrine he proceeded to monopolise her in the most outrageous manner; nor did she refuse to be monopolised. When other people came and tried to talk to her, Desvœux stood by, and contrived to make them feel themselves *de trop*. He put poor Boldero, who flattered

himself that his afternoon's sermon was to
bear good fruit, utterly to the rout ; insulted
General Beau by some absurd question about
the Carraway Islands; put all the aides-de-
camp to flight; and even when the Viceroy
came by and stopped to speak to Maud
seemed to consider it a very great intrusion.

'Really, Mr. Desvœux,' Maud said, with
a laugh, 'you give yourself all the airs of a
jealous husband.'

'I only wish,' said her companion, 'you
had ever given me the chance of being one.
But don't these people bore one ?   I don't
feel a bit inclined to-day to be bored.'

'No more do I,' said Maud, 'but I feel
very cross with you all the same.   Let us go
and sit by the Fotheringhams.'

'Please do not,' said Desvœux; 'here is a
delightful nook, with a smooth stone for your

table, and the stream making too much noise
for anyone to overhear us.   It was evidently
intended for you and me.'

So all the world had the opportunity, at
lunch, of witnessing Desvœux in the act of
adoration ; and, if he would let no one else
have a chance of talking, he had, Maud felt,
plenty to say himself.   It was indiscreet, but
very pleasant.   Even Mrs. Vereker grew
alarmed, and, making an excuse to pass close
by them, came and whispered in Maud's ear
a solemn ' Don't ! '

' Don't what ? ' said Maud, in ill-affected
wonderment.

' Don't be a goose,' said her companion.
' Mr. Desvœux, would you be good-natured
and go and fetch me some ice-pudding,
while I sit and talk to Mrs. Sutton ? '

' With pleasure,' said Desvœux, smothering his resentment as best he could; 'but where am I to sit when I come back?'

'You need not come back for half-an-hour,' said Mrs. Vereker, quietly. 'Go and talk to some one else. I see I must keep you young people both in order.'

Desvœux went off in dudgeon, and Mrs. Vereker lost no time in supplying his place. 'Ah, Mr. Boldero!' she said, 'come and be amusing, please, and give us the latest news from Dustypore.'

For once in his life Boldero thought Mrs. Vereker very nice.

'Be amusing!' thought Maud; 'why does not she ask him to fly to the moon at once? Only Desvœux can be that.'

And so it proved. Even Mrs. Vereker could not make conversation go. Boldero was stiff, uncordial, and ill at ease. Maud

was vexed, and did not care to conceal it.
It was a relief when General Beau appeared,
and Maud, in a pet, asked him to take her to
the waterfall.

The General, who had been intending to
perform the pilgrimage with Mrs. Vereker,
did not betray that he was disconcerted, and
professed his delight at the suggestion.

'But,' said Maud, 'can we trust those
two naughty people together? My dear
Mrs. Vereker, "Don't!"'

'Is not she growing saucy?' Mrs. Vereker
said to Boldero. 'It is all your fault; all you
gentlemen conspire to spoil her.'

'No,' said Boldero, 'begging your
pardon, it is all your fault. You let one of
us have it all his own way. You encourage
him to flirt, and encourage her to encourage
him. It is a shame, Mrs. Vereker—in

another fortnight her reputation will be gone.'

'Fiddlededee!' cried Mrs. Vereker. 'See what jealousy will do! You might as well accuse me of flirting with you; and everyone knows that I am a saint.'

'A very pretty one, and in a very pretty dress,' said Boldero, whom Mrs Vereker's violet eyes always threw off his balance in about two minutes.

'No, thank you,' she said tossing her shapely head in pretty scorn, 'I don't want any flattery; we are too old friends. My dress is lovely, I am well aware, and it has pleased God to make me not quite a fright. But about Maud, now: don't you know that all the gossip is simple envy; some horrid unkind old woman like Mrs. Fotheringham, with about as much heart as one of these rocks, and her two hoydens of girls? But here comes Major Fenton, who has, I consider, quite neglected me to-day.'

Major Fenton was one of the hosts, and the most eligible of the trio.

'Impossible!' he said, melting under the sweet smile from a stern, languid air which he wore to all the world; 'the duties of my day performed, its pleasures are now, I hope, about to begin. Will you come with me to the waterfall?'

Mrs. Vereker bent two soft orbs on Boldero with a reproachful look, as if to say, 'Why did you not ask me sooner?' and went off in glee with the Major; and Boldero, left in solitude to his own meditations, mentally voted this the dullest, flattest, and most unsuccessful picnic at which it had ever been his ill-luck to be a guest.

When Maud and General Beau arrived at the waterfall there, of course, was Desvœux, trying to encourage the Misses Fotheringham to cross the stream, and so ascend to the finest point of view. This was a little more than the Misses Fotheringham's nerves were equal to : the stream was full, and foamed and tossed itself into an angry crest; the water looked black and swift and treacherous. You had to jump on to one boulder, then balance yourself on three stepping-stones through the shallows, then make one good spring to the rock opposite, and the feat was done ! This, however, was just too much for the Misses Fotheringham, who had not been trained in athletics, and were not naturally what the Irishmen call 'leppers.' As they were hesitating and refusing Maud and the General came up, looking very much

bored. Maud had been finding her companion almost intolerable, and would have
jumped *anywhere* to be free of him. There
was nothing in it: Desvœux had been skip-
ping across half-a-dozen times. 'Look,' he
said, 'a skip, two hops and a jump, and
there you are! Do try. Don't you see?'

'I see, exactly,' said Maud, gathering
up her petticoats, and giving her parasol to
General Beau.

'Stop! it is not safe,' he cried. 'Stop,
I implore; the rocks are slippery, the water
is deep. I implore, I beseech, I command!'

But the General might as well have
commanded the stream to stop, for Maud
was gone, and in about two seconds was
standing, flushed, beautiful, and triumphant,
on the opposite side.

'If you will not come with us,' said

Desvœux, calling to the people on the other side, 'we must go up to the Point without you. General Beau will, I am sure, take care of the Misses Fotheringham.'

'A most wilful girl,' thought the General, 'and dull, but a fine jumper, and feet and ankles quite perfection.'

Maud, when she got across the stream, had passed a moral Rubicon ; she left propriety, prudence, and prudishness on the other side with the General and the Misses Fotheringham.

Mr. Desvœux was in the greatest glee at the result which had come about. 'I wish the General had tried, and tumbled in,' he said, 'and got a ducking.'

'Oh,' cried Maud, 'what a dreadful man he is, with his shrugs and his "Ahs !" How lucky that you came to save me !'

'And you to save me,' said her companion. 'I was having a sad time of it with the Misses Fotheringham. What a thing it is to have a deliverer!'

'But,' said Maud, 'I think the younger one is looking very pretty. You know you used to love her. What lovely hair!'

'Yes,' said the other. 'Hair

> 'So young and yellow ; crowning sanctity,
>   And claiming solitude : can hair be false ?'

'It can,' exclaimed Maud; 'Mrs. Blunt showed me two large coils, which had arrived from Douglas in her last box from Europe. When one has a diamond tiara I suppose one must have hair to put it in, *coûte que coûte.*'

'Mrs. Blunt and her eternal tiara!' cried Desvœux: 'like the toad and adversity, ugly and venomous, she wears a precious jewel

in her head. But is not this lovely ? Look
at the rainbow in the foam, and the deep
green of the ferns beside it. Was it not
worth a jump ? '

' Was not *what* worth a jump ? ' said
Maud, with one of her pretty blushes.
' Come Mr. Desvœux, let us get back
before our dear friends have torn us quite
to pieces.'

Maud came back in great spirits, and
made a public laugh at General Beau ' for
his desertion of her.

' " The rocks are slippery, the water is
deep ! " ' she cried, taking him off to his face
with great success. ' " I implore, I entreat,
I command ; but I don't jump ! " O faithless, faithless General Beau ! '

The General was not in the least disconcerted. ' Ah ! ' he said, in his usual

mysterious way ; and everybody felt that he
could have jumped if he had chosen, but
that he had some particular reason for not
choosing to do so.

Then the party re-assembled for tea, and
played at games.   Some one proposed
'What is my thought like?'

'Delightful!' cried Maud. 'General Beau,
what is my thought like, pray?'

'Like?' said the General, quite unprepared for such sudden demands on his con-
versational powers.   'It is like yourself, no
doubt.'

'Enough, enough!' cried Maud.   'Now,
then, please say how wit, which is my word,
and I are like each other?'

'Ah!' said the General, as if to imply
that he mentally perceived the resemblance.
'Because, because——'

'Because,' said Mrs. Vereker, 'you are both to "madness near allied."'

'Or because,' said Desvœux, cutting in with great promptitude, '"free wit is nature to advantage dressed;" and so, I am sure, is Mrs. Sutton.'

'Very nice!' cried Maud, glowing with pleasure. 'Now, General Beau, you must pay forfeit, you know. I will give you a bad one for deserting me so cruelly.'

'Forfeits!' said Desvœux. 'Spare us, spare us—they are too fatiguing.'

'Not a bit,' said Maud. 'You bow to what is wisest, and kneel to what is prettiest, and kiss what you love best.'

'Well, then,' said Desvœux, kissing his hand sentimentally, and blowing it into the air, 'there is a kiss for what I love best, wherever it may be.'

'Dear me,' said Mrs. Vereker, 'what a touching idea! There goes my kiss!'

'And,' cried Maud, laughing and kissing the tips of her pretty fingers, 'there goes mine! What a state the air will be in! But here comes Major Fenton with a plate of plumcake, which is what I love best; so my kiss is for that!'

'Happy plumcake!' said the Major, gallantly, 'to be loved, eaten, and kissed by a mouth so fair.'

'Give me a bit too, Fenton,' said Desvœux. 'I must eat some for sympathy, though it is not what I love best.'

Then the quiet valley shadows crept about them, and it grew sad and sombre, and while they sat and talked and laughed the day was done, and all steps were turned towards home.

So Maud and Desvœux found themselves travelling home together in the moonlight, and falling behind the crowd of riders, to enjoy, undisturbed, the pleasure of a tête-à-tête. One of the great dangers of the Hills is that the paths admit only of two people riding abreast ; the *terzo incommodo* must ride behind, and might, so far as prudence is concerned, just as well not be there at all. No such inconvenient intruder, however, threatened Desvœux's enjoyment of the present occasion, or aided the faltering monitions which Maud's half-silenced conscience whispered to her. Her nerves were utterly overstrung, and the excessive loveliness of the scene seemed only to add to her excitement. Along the winding path which crept up the mountain-side, and through the dark green forest-trees towering sublimely

over them, and all ablaze in moonlit
patches with silver floods of light, their
journey took them. Far away, miles below,
a hundred tiny sparks showed where the
villagers were cooking the evening meal;
and across the valley, on the opposite side,
a great streak of woodland was blazing,
scarcely seen by day, but now a ruddy lurid
glow in the white light that lit up all the
scene around. In the horizon the great,
cold, snowy range, standing out hard and
clear in the moonlight, still, majestic, awful.
How sweet, how bright, how exhilarating to
a heart so prompt for enjoyment, senses
so quickly impressible, nerves so alive to
every surrounding influence as Maud's!
Again and again she burst into exclamations
of pleasure as each turn in the road brought
them to some new scene of enchantment.

'Let us stop,' she cried. 'I must get off and sit down here and enjoy this in peace.'

'Let us walk a little,' said Desvœux, 'and send our ponies on to await us at the half-way point. Are you too tired?'

'I am not a bit tired,' Maud said, glowing with pleasure; 'it is too lovely to think of it. This is the best of all the day's pleasures.'   .

'It is lovely,' said her companion, 'but to me its greatest charm is that I have you to myself.'

'Well,' said Maud, who was accustomed to pulling up Desvœux when he became inconveniently sentimental, 'we have had a delightful day, and great fun. I wish we had had the forfeits all the same, and made General Beau do something nice. You stopped it all, Mr. Desvœux, by being so idle. Why did you blow your kiss into the air ? '

' It was the only thing I could do with it,' said Desvœux ; ' and see, it has alighted on your cheek ! '

' And *that* on your arm,' cried Maud, wielding her whip with a sudden vehemence which made Desvœux feel that his kiss had been, at any rate, well paid for. ' When I want to be kissed I will tell you, but no robberies ! '

' You little spitfire ! ' said Desvœux, rubbing his shoulder with a comic air.

' Well,' said Maud, suddenly repentant, and trying her whip across her knee, ' it *does* hurt, I confess. I beg your pardon. You deserved it, however, and I was in a passion at the moment. Do you forgive me ?' She gave him her hand—that little, delicate, exquisitely-fashioned piece of Nature's workmanship, which Desvœux had often vowed was the most beautiful thing in India. Its very touch electrified him.

'Forgive you?' he said, with a sudden sadness in his voice. 'You hurt me once in good earnest, and I forgave you that, and do forgive it, but it hurts me still.'

Desvœux's voice trembled with feeling. Something in his look struck Maud with a sudden pang of pity, sympathy, remorse. Was Desvœux then really suffering, and his life darkened on account of her? She stooped towards him, bent her cheek, flushed with excitement, to his, pressed to his the lips on which Desvœux's thoughts had dwelt a hundred times in impassioned reverie, and kissed him with a long, sweet,

earnest caress, the sudden outburst of gratitude, tenderness, regret.

Desvœux said not a word, but he still
kept possession of her hand, and the two
stood looking silently across the misty valley
and the precipice that fell away at their feet
into solemn gloom below. The tramp of a
horse's feet was heard behind them, and
Boldero came trotting innocently up the
path.

'We are walking home,' Maud said, 'the
night is so delicious. You may get off and
come with us, if you please.'

Boldero, who would have jumped over
the mountain-side if Maud had bidden him,
at once dismounted ; Desvœux fell behind,
and said not one word during the rest of the
homeward journey.

CHAPTER XXXVII.

ILL NEWS FLY APACE.

Never any more, while I live,
Need I hope to see his face as before.

MAUD reached her house over-tired, over-
wrought, and somewhat sad at heart. She
had gone much further than she meant, much
further than her real feelings prompted.
Even as she yielded to the sudden impulse
she had repented, and while still doing it
begun to wish the deed undone. She had
been vexed and teased and excited till she
scarce knew what her actions meant. The
man to whom she had committed herself by
so compromising an indiscretion had no

sooner reached the dangerous eminence in her regard than he began to fall away, and make her doubly remorseful for the act. She resented his ascendency over her, the force of the liking with which he inspired her, and the degree to which he led her where he would. His language, when he was not there to carry it off with fun and daring, seemed unreal, exaggerated, absurd. Even before they got home her taste had begun to turn against him. Boldero's almost reverential care of her set her upon disparaging the other's lawless, inconsiderate homage. The very way in which he stayed behind was, she knew, intended as a sulky protest against Boldero's intrusion. A man who really cared about her would, Maud felt, have acquiesced in what she chose, what it was obviously right for her to choose,

without any such display of temper. Then
there had been something in Desvœux's
manner, when he wished her good-night,
which implied a private understanding, and
set her heart beating with indignation. A
really fine nature would have been doubly
deferential, doubly courteous, doubly watch-
ful against seeming to take a liberty. Desvœux's tone had something in it, to Maud's
ear, which was familiar, easy, only just not
disrespectful. She had been defying public
opinion for him all day; she had at last, in a
sudden impulse of pity, put herself at his
mercy, and she began to doubt whether he
was a man who would use his advantage
generously. Perhaps after all Felicia had
been right about him.

Then, when she got home, everything
conspired to try her nerves. In the first

place, no letter had come from her husband ; there had been no letter for two days before, and this was a longer interval than had ever yet occurred. She tried in vain not to be frightened at the unaccustomed silence. Mrs. Vereker laughed her anxieties to scorn, but Maud knew better what such a long cessation implied. Her conscience was too ill at ease not to be apprehensive at the first occasion, however trivial, for alarm. Either something had happened or, dreadful possibility, her husband was displeased, and too displeased to write. While she was taking off her things and harassing herself with all sorts of fancied troubles, Mrs. Vereker came in and completed her discomfiture.

'Maud,' she said, and Maud thought

her tones sounded harsh and unsympathetic (how different from Felicia's gentle lectures! which always thawed her heart at once), ' I have been commissioned to give you a scolding, and by whom, do you suppose ? '

' I really don't know, and don't care,' said Maud, in a pet. ' I have had enough the last few days to last me for some time. Will it not keep till to-morrow or the day after ? '

' No, it will not,' said Mrs. Vereker, who was herself sincerely provoked at the notoriety which Maud's indiscretion had attained. ' It is from the Viceroy. I have something to say to you from him. Now do you wish to hear ? '

' No,' said Maud, 'unless it is an appointment for my husband.'

' No, but it is about your husband, or about things your husband would not like. He told me to scold you thoroughly.'

' Then,' said Maud, her heart beating so that she could scarcely speak, ' he took a great liberty. I know, however, that he did not.'

' Guilty conscience !' cried the other. ' How white you look ! Well, it is not exactly the truth, but it is not far off it. He gave me a hint.'

' He gave you a fiddlestick!' cried Maud, in a passion. ' He meant to tell you not to flirt yourself.'

' Oh ! no ; Lord Clare and I understand each other far too well for that. He said quite seriously, " When is Colonel Sutton coming up ? Why don't he come ? He ought to come ; write to him and say so ; say so from me." Now, what do you think that meant ? '

Maud felt her colour gone, and her heart beating violently, and could venture on no reply.

'You see,' said her monitress, pitilessly, 'you will be injudicious. I am always telling you. You can't be content with fluttering round the candle, but must needs go into the flame and singe your wings, and then of course it hurts you. People should know when to stop.'

'And,' cried Maud, in a thorough passion, 'people should not throw stones who live in glass houses. Why, Mrs. Vereker, if I am a flirt, I should like to know who taught me ? '

'Now you are rude and cross. You should never throw stones, whether you live in a glass house or not. The best thing I can do is to leave you to recover your temper.'

Mrs. Vereker was gone, and Maud's last friend seemed lost to her. She had offended everyone; or rather everyone had done something to offend her. She disliked them all. She flung herself upon her bed and wept in very bitterness of heart. She longed for a really friendly, loving hand to take her and set her right; she longed for her old mistress to confess to; she thought of Felicia, considerate, tender, sympathetic, and she seemed like an angel compared with those amongst whom she was living. If she could but have crept to her embrace, and breathed her troubles in her ear! She thought of her husband; the pure and faithful heart beating with no thought but for her, where nothing coarse or unchivalrous could ever find a place; where she knew that she alone was enshrined; of his perfect trust in her, his spotless faith, his transparent honour. She looked at his photograph standing on the table: how grave and sad it looked! She flung herself on the bed; the bitter tears of remorse and repentance began to flow, and while they flowed—for Maud was far more exhausted than she knew—she slept; and in her sleep of a few minutes passed into dreamland; not the happy, silly, aimless dreamland of easy minds and tired frames, where Maud's nights were chiefly spent; but into a sad weird region, where everything seemed horribly real and con- nected and designed, and to bear some frightful relation to actual life that makes it part of our being, and haunts one's afterthoughts. She was with her husband once again, and yet it was not quite himself; an undefined something separated him from her and all the past. She was riding by him. How grieved and reproachful a mien he wore, as of a man with a hidden sorrow cankering his heart! And then he fell, and Maud saw him crushed and wounded and helpless as once before, and agonised in some frightful entanglement with his horse. She meanwhile was trying in vain to help or to approach him, for a hidden hand restrained her, and Sutton himself, sad and stern, was waving her away. And then came a fierce struggle, and blows and cries, and Maud found herself waking with a scream, and her servant standing by her bed and saying that a 'Sahib' had come, and wanted to see her directly.

She knew what it meant, and went with a beating heart into the drawing-room, as fresh from the land of sorrow, and ready for news of disaster.

She found Boldero in the drawing-room, looking ominously grave.

'Well, Mr. Boldero,' Maud said, with an unsuccessful attempt at gaiety, and a dread of the answer which she would receive, ' why have you come back ? Do you want me to give you some tea, or to receive some advice ? '

' Have you heard from Sutton to-day ? ' said the other, not heeding her enquiry.

' No,' said Maud, turning sick at heart and deadly white. ' Why do you ask ? Quick, quick ! '

' Because I have bad accounts of him from Dustypore. You must not be alarmed.'

'But I *am* alarmed,' cried Maud, by this time in thorough terror. 'Don't you see that standing there and giving hints is just the way to frighten one? I know quite well you have brought me some bad news.'

'Yes,' said Boldero, 'I am sorry to say I have. Your husband is ill.'

Maud started up and looked him straight in the face, with a serious, eager look, that made Boldero, even at that moment, think how lovely she was.

'Now,' she cried, 'tell me the truth. Have you told me all?'

'No, I have not. I can hardly bear to tell you; but you have sense and courage, and would rather hear the truth. *He is down with cholera.*'

The words went like a sword through Maud's heart. A blank horror seized her.

This, then, had been the meaning of her dream. The blow came crashing down upon her, and body and soul seemed to reel before it. She sank like a crushed, terrified child on the sofa, and, covering her face in her hands, hid herself, speechless, motionless, as from an ill that was too great to bear.

'Let me send for Mrs. Vereker,' said Boldero.

'No!' cried Maud, starting up, 'pray do not. Leave me for a minute or two. I shall be better directly. Will you come back in a quarter of an hour?'

'I will do anything you bid me,' said Boldero, frightened at the task he had in hand and its probable results, and thinking that perhaps the best thing he could do was to leave Maud to deal with her sorrow alone.

So Boldero went out into the moonlight

and strolled about the pathway, now so silent, where so many joyous footsteps used to press, and Maud was left to herself with her first great trouble.

It was significant of the real nature of her relations to Mrs. Vereker that she shrank especially from seeking her now, in her time of sorrow, or following her counsel. Mrs. Vereker was essentially a fine-weather friend. The task which Maud had now in hand was something deeper and graver than anything that the other's feelings reached. What lay before her now to do, or to endure, was something between her husband and herself, and it would be profanity for a stranger to come into that sacred region. Mrs. Vereker's advice would, Maud knew instinctively, be all wrong. She herself felt already what she ought to do. She knelt weeping on the sofa,

and the thoughts of sorrow, humiliation,
remorse, came pouring thick upon her
troubled mind. To what a precipice's edge
had not her folly and madness brought her!
her fair fame darkened, her husband's name
dishonoured, her vows of love and honour
how badly kept! Oh, how unutterably weak,
faithless, heartless she had been! How
ghastly all the afternoon's adventures, the
evening's folly, seemed! how wicked, how
base, how altogether bad! She had felt the
thought stinging all the while, but other,
stronger feelings had helped her to ignore it
and forget. Now there was no other feeling,
and it was overwhelming.

There was only one thing left to do, one
good, one hope left, to fly to her husband's
side, to pour out the pent-up stream of
confession, repentance, and love, and, if only

God would spare him, never,, never leave him again!

When Boldero came in again Maud was herself again. 'I am better and stronger now,' she said; 'the news came upon me too suddenly; but now I am calm. I have settled what I ought to do, and you must help me. I shall go down to him at once.'

'Indeed you cannot do that,' Boldero said, decisively; 'it would be excessively wrong.'

'Indeed, indeed I will!' cried Maud. 'I feel that I ought and must. What is there to stop me?'

'It is out of the question,' said the other. 'You will be running into a great deal of danger unnecessarily.'

'I have no strength to talk about it,' said Maud, 'but I must go or I shall die, and you must help me. Do you mean me to stay quietly here, and Jem dying by himself? My God, my God! why did I ever leave him?'

Here Maud threw herself on the sofa and cried a longer, sadder, more heartfelt cry than ever in her life before. Boldero went again into the garden in despair, for it was in vain, he saw, to try to soothe her.

It ended, of course, in Boldero telegraphing for two relays of horses to be sent out from the Camp, and sending out two more as fast as possible, to get as far as might be on the way for the forced march of fifty miles which Maud and he were, it was settled, at once to undertake. She was to rest for a few hours, start at three o'clock, get on as far as they could in the cool, rest through the day, and complete the remainder of the journey the following night. They would be at the Camp, Boldero thought, by the morning of the day after to-morrow.

It required all his official resources to organise such a journey, but a Collector on his march can do anything; and Boldero, with whom Maud was rapidly mounting up from heroine to saint, was determined that her journey, so far as in him lay, should be as comfortable as money and care could make it.

CHAPTER XXXVIII.

FLIGHT.

In old days there were angels who came and took men
by the hand, and led them away from the City of Destruction. We see no white-winged angels now; but yet men are
led away from threatening destruction : a hand is put into
theirs, which leads them gently towards a calm and bright
land, so that they look no more backward.

MAUD effected a speedy reconciliation with
Mrs. Vereker, who had entrenched herself
in her bedroom with a French novel till
such time as Maud should have recovered
her equanimity. Mrs. Vereker at once
forgot her grievance, listened with real
concern to Maud's alarming tidings, and
lent herself with great alacrity to assist in
the preparations for a hasty departure.

Boldero had gone off, and was to get coolies together as speedily as possible, so as to be well on the way during the cool hours of the early morning, before the heat of the day would render travelling a work of distress.

By three o'clock, accordingly, a little army was collected in front of Mrs. Vereker's door. The urgent demands of the Collector and the subsequent zeal of the Tehsildar had done wonders, and some forty men had been assembled at a moment's notice for the task of carrying down Maud, her servant, and her various belongings.

The moon had sunk, and the torches glared fitfully with dreadful smell and smoke. The figures looked weird and strange, and, to Maud's eye, horribly numerous. The arrangement of each box involved enormous discussion as to how the burden of carrying it could best be shared. At last all was ready; Maud was established in a palanquin, the carriers kept time to the cadence of a wild refrain, the torch-bearers shuffled along in front, relays of coolies came behind; close at her side rode the faithful Boldero, marshalling the little force, and ever on the watch to shield her from any possible annoyance. Maud appreciated his fidelity, and felt that she had never liked him half well enough before. Her conscience smote her for all her rude speeches, slighting acts, and unkind looks; she determined henceforth to be very kind indeed. Boldero, accordingly, though in a great state of agitation and distress about his friend's condition, found the journey not quite without its charm.

He had telegraphed to the Camp for Sutton's horses to be sent out, and both of

them were well accustomed to carry Maud
when occasion offered.   A messenger was to
be sent up to each halting-place, so that
Maud had not an hour longer to wait for
news than was absolutely necessary.   It was
a relief, hour by hour, to find the distance
growing less and the messages more recent;
still the tidings were very grievous.   Sutton,
it was clear, was very ill.   He had been
thoroughly knocked up beforehand, and agitated and distressed about something, the
doctors thought, and this no doubt had
helped the evil.   This was a cruel stab for
Maud.   For a few days, said the letter, it
would be rash to say what turn the case
might take ; still there was reason to be
hopeful—he was a very strong man, and
very temperate, and these points, of course,
were greatly in his favour.   The mortality,

however, had been terrible at the Camp, and the men were greatly disheartened. They were now marching every day, in hopes of keeping clear of their own infection. An hour or two later the two travellers came to a halt. Maud found some early tea awaiting her, and joyfully exchanged the tiring captivity of the palanquin for the horse which had been hurried on for her use for this stage of the journey.

'I have been fast asleep,' she said, 'as Boldero and she rode down the hillside together, and watched the faint glow in the east warming gradually into day, 'and this is very refreshing. The darkness, the crowd, the blazing torches, the confusion, the babel of tongues we had last night seem like a horrid dream. I was never more thankful for the light. I feel as if I were

escaping; and, Mr. Boldero, you are my
deliverer. I shall be grateful to you all my
life. You must have had so much trouble,
and have done it all so kindly and like yourself.'

'Do not talk of that,' said the other.
'What are friends for but to serve us when
we need them?'

'And to forgive us when we wrong
them?' said Maud, whose conscience was
goading her to confession. 'I know I have
behaved ill to you—to you and to everybody.
Now I am going to try to do better, if only
I can get the chance—if only God in his
goodness will grant me that.'

'I am hopeful,' said Boldero, 'for both of
you. Sutton, I feel, has something greater
yet to do. We have often laughed and said
that nothing can kill him. You know in

cholera it is as much mind as body: courage, calmness, and determination are half the battle.'

'Then,' said Maud, with enthusiasm, faith and hopefulness glowing in her face, 'I am sure he will do well. His body is his soul's servant; you cannot fancy how completely it does its bidding as a matter of course. I do not think it would even die without his leave. Have you telegraphed to say that I am coming?'

'Yes, but leaving it to the doctors to tell him when they think best; or not at all, if they fear the intelligence will excite him. Very likely they will be afraid to do so.'

'They will do wrong,' said Maud, who knew her husband's temperament better even than Boldero. 'It will not agitate him, and it will make him resolve to live. He *will*

live, I believe, if it is only in order to forgive me.'

'Do not say "to forgive," said the other,
who, in a generous reaction of sentiment,
began to think that Maud was pressing with
undue severity against herself; 'to tell you
all that you have been to him, and all the
sunshine you have brought into his life.'

'All I have been!' cried Maud, with a
vehement remorse. 'I could tell him that
best. You could tell him. I mean to tell
him the first moment I can—and I am in an
agony till I can do so. I have been mad,
Mr. Boldero, or in a dream, I think, and you
tried in vain to wake me. Now I am awake,
and know the truth. All the things and
people we have left behind are merely
shadows, and I mistook them for realities;
only one thing in the world is real for me:

my love for my husband. Other people
flatter and excite and amuse one, and one
is carried away with all sorts of follies; but
my heart never moves and never can. It is
his and his only, and I never knew it fully
till last night. My life, I find, is centred in
his.'

'I pray God,' said Boldero, devoutly, 'we
may find him better; and somehow I believe
we shall.'

A level stretch of valley lay before them,
and allowed them to push sharply over the
next five or six miles. By ten o'clock they
arrived at their halting-place, where Boldero
proposed that they should wait till the afternoon. Maud, however, was too restless to
halt.

'Suppose,' she said, 'we push on another

stage ?   The sun is not so very dreadful, after all.'

' The next two stages arc bad ones,' said Boldero.   ' Don't you remember that long, troublesome valley with the rocks on either side ?—by twelve o'clock they will be all red-hot.'

'Well,' said Maud, 'we will tie a wet towel over my head.   Will it do you any harm ?   or the horses ?'

' Me !' cried Boldero, in a tone which at once reassured his companion that no danger need be apprehended so far as he was con-cerned.   'As for my horses, they can, of course, go as many stages as you like.'

So they dressed and breakfasted, and Maud declared herself quite ready for an immediate start.   Boldero brought in a great plantain-leaf rom the garden of the little inn,

and they tied this under her wide pith hat ;
then Maud armed herself with an enormous
umbrella, and 'Now,' she said, ' I am prepared for anything.'

By the end of the stage, however, her
strength was spent—she sank into the first
chair that offered itself, and acquiesced
thankfully, like a tired child, in Boldero's
decision that they should not move again till
the day's fierce glare was past. There was
no need to hurry, for she was now within a
night's march of her husband, and by the
morrow's morning would have known and
seen the worst.

CHAPTER XXXIX.

THE PRODIGAL'S RETURN.

Thus 'twas granted me
To know he loved me to the depth and height
Of such large natures, ever competent
With grand horizons, by the land or sea,
To love's grand sunrise.   Small spheres hold small fires,
But he loved largely.

MAUD was inexpressibly shocked at her husband's appearance. Neither the telegrams, nor the doctor's notes, nor Boldero's description had in the faintest degree prepared her for what she saw. She had heard of Death, and even seen it, but in its gentle, peaceful, unagonised aspect; she had seen illness, but in its milder mood, as it visits the

European household: not the savage, des-
troying, desolating demon-angel that waves
a sword across the cholera-stricken plain or
city in the East. A sickness of a few days,
a few hours, shatters the sufferer's frame,
blurs out the familiar features, leaves the
stalwart man a quivering skeleton, deadens
the sense, and clouds the strong mind with a
deep, dreadful shadow of oblivion.

And to this stage Sutton had come.
Maud, despite all entreaties and warnings,
went straight to her husband's side and let
the full horror of the scene take possession of
her soul. It wrung her very heart to see
him ; the man whom, after all, she loved
with a passion which, if sometimes forgotten,
was never extinct for an instant. She had
loved him at first ; she loved him now ten
times more than ever. She had wronged

him, neglected him, dishonoured him—alas, how grievously!—her one hope lay in con- fession, reconciliation, forgiveness, and he lay there, more dead than alive, speechless, motionless, except when some spasm of suffering shook him, and, so far as outward sign showed, unconscious of her presence. Maud thanked Heaven that she was on the spot to know and see the worst, and yet it was almost more than she could bear.   Her load of anguish seemed too much for one till now a stranger to sorrow.   Again and again some old trait in the haggard, suffering face, a moan of pain, a gesture too slight from weakness to be intelligible to any eye but hers, touched a fresh chord in her heart, broke down her wavering fortitude, and sent her rushing to her room to shed in solitude the tears of sorrow and remorse.   Again and again she washed away the useless tears, nerved herself once more to maintain a courageous exterior, and returned, with a fortitude which she felt gather strength within her, to the sad task of watching and waiting for the crisis which a few hours more must bring.

Let us leave that terrible passage of Maud's life, with its trembling, agonising suspense, its heartfelt vows and prayers, its remorseful tears, its thrilling hopes, its mysterious communings with another world. Let us drop a curtain over that solemn season : Maud will emerge from it, we may be sure, with a new-born fortitude, patience, loftiness of soul: courage, the child of suffering : calmness, the attribute of those who have been close upon despair.

A fortnight later Sutton was lying in the

drawing-room, with no other malady than excessive weakness, and with no other occupation than to recruit his shattered powers. Maud was busied with the composition of some appetising beverage which was, the doctor said, the only kind of medicine of which he now stood in need, and which could, in Maud's and her husband's opinion, be properly concocted and administered by no hand but hers. Then the invalid's pillows needed skilful arrangement, for he was still at the stage when mere lying still is an exertion which seems to tax every limb and muscle in the aching frame. Maud found an indescribable relief and pleasure in waiting on her husband, and, no doubt, proved herself an adept in the kindly art of nursing. Every act (though her husband knew it not) had, to Maud's aching conscience, a sort of penitential devotion about it, and said a hundred things of love and sorrow which as yet found no utterance in spoken words.

'What a model wife !' said Sutton, as he lay watching her movements, in grateful admiration at her skill and care on his behalf.

' Ah ! but,' said Maud, thankful for the opportunity of the confession she was longing to make, ' I am not a model wife at all, but just everything that a model ought not to be.'

' Then,' said Jem, gallantly, ' I am for you, and not for the model, whoever drew it.'

' Jem,' she said, with sudden seriousness, ' I want to tell you something, and be forgiven. I meant to do so before, but you have been too poorly. I am afraid it will hurt you. I have been going on very stupidly at Elysium, and very wrongly, and doing everything that you would most have disliked, and that I dislike now—oh! how bitterly!'

Sutton, to Maud's great relief, did not seem in the least surprised or inclined to be serious about the matter. He took her hand and held it with the kindest caressing manner.

·'I have no doubt,' he said, 'that Mrs. Vereker did all she could to get you into a scrape. It was a shame of me to let you go to her.'

'No,' said Maud, 'it was not her fault at all. The truth is, I have been flirting with—some.one.'

'Some one,' said Sutton, 'has been trying to flirt with you, you mean, and no wonder. Some one showed his good taste at any rate.'

'Yes, but,' said the penitent, 'I flirted with him. I think I must have been crazy.'

'You risked your life, dear, to come and be with me. Why look further back than that? I cannot.'

'But,' said Maud, her cheeks burning scarlet at the awful confession which conscience compelled her to make, 'that is not all : *I gave him a kiss.*'

'Then,' said her husband, 'you gave him a great deal more than he deserved, whoever he was. Well, now, give me one, and let us say no more about it.'

The blinding tears fell fast and hot as Maud bent over her husband's haggard face and exchanged the sweet pledge of reconciliation, confidence, and love. There was something so generous, sparing, and delicately magnanimous in her husband's ready, unenquiring forgiveness, and his refusal to know more of a matter which it grieved and shamed her to narrate. Maud knew that his was a temperament which jealousy would torture like any Othello's, and that his passion against an offender, had it once forced its way to light, would have been a sort of fury. She could perfectly realise to herself her husband doing anything—the worst—to a man who, he thought, had in the slightest degree wronged him. He was accustomed to stern deeds and stern sights, and, as any man does who has a hundred times seen death face to face and found nothing to dread in it, held life the cheapest of all his treasures. Maud had felt an awful misgiving lest he should utter some dreadful, quiet threat at the wrong-doer. As it was, her husband

would not even know his name, and treated
the whole thing as a mere childish mis-
adventure. It was indeed an heroic kindness. Her whole nature went out to him
in thankfulness and love ; she bent her head
beside him, and hid her face and wept in the
fulness of her heart. No wonder his soldiers
had learnt to worship him. No word more
was spoken, but Sutton had good cause to
know that the last touch of waywardness, the
last fickle mood, the forgetful moment, the
girlish caprice, were gone for ever—the last
spot in her heart that had not been wholly his
was carried at last. 'I am thankful,' the
surgeon said, 'that he is better : the poor
child is ten times more in love with him
than ever.'

Then the three friends had a very happy
time. It is so pleasant to be getting well ;

and nursing, too, is a pleasant labour, when the invalid is interesting and considerate and well-beloved. Happy the patient whose lot it is to pass from the dreary land of sickness with such sweet companionship! Boldero, though the gravity of his loss kept pace in his thoughts with each new-discovered charm in Maud, got himself into an heroic mood, and derived a satisfaction less blackened with melancholy than he would have conceived possible from the sight of his friend's felicity. At any rate he made himself very pleasant—was always available for whatever was wanted of him; submitted, it is probable, to a little delightful tyranny from the woman he adored, and went away at last, leaving almost a little blank behind him.

'How kind and useful he has been!' Maud said, as they watched his cavalcade winding along the valley; 'and how clever about your barley-water! Yes—I certainly like him.'

'Like him!' said Sutton. 'I should think so. He is the best fellow in the world.'

'Yes,' said his wife, 'all the same there is something pleasant in a tête-à-tête; and I don't like anybody taking care of you but me.'

L'ENVOI.

Hope, which catches up the brush as it falls from the narrator's hand, adds yet another scene in the faint, hazy, indistinct‿hues of a distant horizon to the picture at which we have been looking for awhile.

We are on Aldershot Heath. Troops are marching up from different directions ; orderlies are galloping wildly on their behests ; words of command ring noisily through the air ; great masses of red come looming out of the dust as each regiment tramps solidly along ; there is the roar of cannon from the neighbouring hill ; the horse artillery goes rattling by like a hurricane of horses and iron; in front is a long array of spectators, and in the midst a blaze of uniforms and the carriage where a gracious Sovereign sits to inspect and compliment the heroes of the day—the men who have served their country well; for there has been a successful expedition, led by an Indian General; and the victorious army, with its leader, bearing his honours thick upon him, at its head, is marching past amidst the shouts of a joyful and sympathetic crowd. When Sutton, for it is he, has passed the Royal carriage and made his salute, he turns his horse and joins the staff who glitter round their Sovereign. Kind words are spoken, and a Royal hand adds one more to his long list of decorations. Presently he makes his way to a group of ladies in a carriage near at hand. There is

Felicia, with a sweet, matronly air, her beautiful features none the less fair for the lines that sorrow has left upon them and some silvery threads among the waving gold ; she sits serene and joyous in the presence of two lovely girls, Sutton's playfellows of old, now, as he tells them, when he wants to be very polite, the very repetition of their mother. Vernon is in England, at home for his last furlough, and beyond lies, near enough now to be a source of pleasure, not of pain, the prospect of a final settlement at home. Beside Felicia sits Maud, blushing under her husband's honours, but rejoicing that all the world should recognise his claim to homage. As he comes up the smile that she gives him tells us that all is more than well between them. Suddenly she jumps up with an exclamation, for she has recognised a familiar face—it is Boldero, who is making his way to them through the crowd. He brings a blushing lady on his arm, and he is blushing too, and there are introductions and greetings which sound as if his old love-wound had been healed by the only effectual remedy.

Meanwhile the long armed array is flowing steadily past. Maud, who is quite the soldier's wife, criticises and approves. At length the last regiment has come and gone, the last band has crashed out its music, the Royal carriage makes a move, the staff gallops away, the crowd is pushing and hurrahing and scattering itself over the wide plain ; the shades of evening are gathering over it ; the Indian friends drive off merrily for home ; the scene fades—fades and dies away.

Let us leave this party of happy people to themselves—we must be their companions no longer.

THE END.

LONDON : PRINTED BY
SPOTTISWOODE AND CO., NEW-STREET SQUARE
AND PARLIAMENT STREET